Love, Chocolates
and Medicine

Love, Chocolates and Medicine

Dr. Ravi Shekhar Krishna

authorHOUSE®

AuthorHouse™
1663 Liberty Drive
Bloomington, IN 47403
www.authorhouse.com
Phone: 1-800-839-8640

Published by AuthorHouse   10/31/2012

ISBN: 978-1-4772-4348-0 (sc)
ISBN: 978-1-4772-4350-3 (hc)
ISBN: 978-1-4772-4349-7 (e)

CONTENTS

Chapter One

"OMG, THE RESULTS ARE OUT!"

It was a perfect evening. Mom and Dad had gone out for some work. I and Aditi were sitting in the middle of the garden playing with the new Pomeranian puppy I had bought her after our engagement. I know a stupid present, but I wanted to give her something that would last long or if not at least his memories would. She loved the puppy as if it was her own baby. It was just the two of us, and of course the puppy but he didn't really have the brains to understand what actually was going inside my heart. Unfortunately neither did Aditi, or at least that's what I thought.

We were definitely enjoying each other's company sitting in the midst of dark green grass all around, the light green golden hetch at the edges giving it a perfect contrast, those several rows of blossoming roses adding to its beauty, with the white and light blue walls behind matching perfectly with the sky. To talk about the sky, it was perfectly blue, the kind of shade you would fall in love with, with a few scattered clouds here and there. We could see fleets of birds flying to their destinations. The sun was going down on far west and so was my heart as there were no hopes of anything happening. I had the girl of my dreams sitting right next to me. I could just open my arms and engulf her into my love. But wouldn't it be too soon? I mean we were just engaged. And she wasn't making any moves either.

I was struggling to think what to do when to my rescue God sent the rain. It was like a blessing. The puppy was the first one to hop his way into the house. We stood up together to make our run. And as soon as I reached under the shed I noticed it was just the two of us standing there, me and the puppy. I looked up only to realize that in front of me was standing the most beautiful creation of God.

She just stood there in her blue jeans and white t shirt getting wet in the rain. She had such a cute face, those beautiful big eyes with a cute little nose, her smooth pink lips that would make any one lose control, her body, those curves, as if they were made only to make me go insane. And the way drops of water were making their way from the tip of her hair on to her body driving up and downhill finally to blend perfectly with the grass, it was making me sweat.

The rain was getting heavier but she didn't move an inch in spite of my many attempts to call her in. She was staring straight at me with those beautiful eyes as if they were saying something. I had started to lose it. It was getting out of control. Out of desperation I said "Come on in or I'm coming to get you."

She turned away from me and in a very naughty but soothing voice said "Come get me."

That was it. I jumped into the rain and within the next blink of her eyes I was standing right next to her, very close, touching her. I turned her around to hug her so tight. After a few moments she moved back, looked deep into my eyes and then placed a kiss on my forehead, then on my eyes and then on my cheeks and then, and then my world just stood still for a second. Our lips met, oh those soft sweet lips. Even without saying a word she had said everything that my heart wanted to hear. I knew it was going to happen. Love was going to happen. Within seconds we were on the grass, but this time not on our feet. We were laying right next to each other, or rather over each other, hugging and kissing each other when I decided to go down on her. She started exclaiming Himanshu! Himanshu! HIMANSHU!! HIMANSHU!! She screamed my name only to scream louder and louder.

But wait. Why was she sounding like my dad, wait, what???

"Himanshu! Who the hell do you think you are, sleeping this late in the morning? Its 10 am already. Get up; don't you want to know how you have disappointed me in your exams??"

It was the day my exam results were supposed to come out and my dad was sprinkling water over me trying to wake me up. In a split second the rain was gone. The puppy was gone, my love, my romance, my Aditi was gone.

It was the 10th of February already, almost 15 days past my last university exams and all I could remember was to eat and sleep. And if I wasn't lazy enough I would go out for a movie or so. Most of my school friends were not even available any more. Either they were in college or had shifted to some other city. Half of them even had jobs already. MBBS is a really long course you know; during mine I never really realized when others graduated and when they were up on their own feet.

My Dad's extra polite way of waking me up did work and I was up. Though still a little drowsy, somehow I managed to drag my ass of the bed to the wash room. In less than 20 minutes I was somewhat ready wearing a lose t-shirt and shorts. I picked up my phone to check for a message that I was waiting for but it showed none. This was when my mom walked in, the extra superstitious kind of person who believes in God beyond crazy and like every other mom, is a cleanliness freak.

"What is this??" She asked.

"What is what?" I wasn't sure of what she was asking.

"This?" She said pointing at my shorts.

One of our family friends was invited today for lunch. Now how was I supposed to know that? Anyways I changed into jeans instead of the shorts, and went straight to the kitchen. Obviously I was hungry.

Mom was cooking lunch for the guests when I interrupted her.

"So what's for breakfast??"

"Breakfast at noon?" She asked.

"Why not?" I said shrugging my shoulders.

She just turned away getting back to what she was cooking. I opened up the fridge searching for something to eat when she spoke again.

"Please don't drop anything. Please don't increase my work. Your breakfast is on the dining table already. Go get it!!"

I rushed to the dining room. On the table was kept a plate covered with another. I opened it to find 3 parathas and an omelette, the kind I like, with spring onions and baby corn. Why do Moms have to be like this? I mean she could have been sweet with me and just told me in the first place. But no, they have to be rude and harsh and dramatic, and then slowly reveal that they love us more than we could love ourselves.

I finished my breakfast in a hurry and soon was in front of my laptop in my room, yes it was time for the result. Before typing in the site's address I said few words, like God please help me this time and I swear I'll be a nice guy with girls and that I'll be more responsible from now on. All this time I could see my mom peeping into the room to see if something good or bad had happened already. There were calls from dad every 15 minutes to find if the results were out.

I kept my phone by the side of my computer and finally typed in the address and hit Enter. It was processing. Of what I can remember I was never so tensed in my entire life.

The results were not out yet. It said "results under processing". I knew I had to wait for some time before I disappointed my parents. I was dying out of tension. I decided to log into Facebook. To my relief most of my friends, Rahul, Suraj, Anand, Nitin, Suman, almost the whole batch was online. Of course it was the day results were coming out.

We all started chatting, about all kinds of stuff. What are the new movies? Which new bike is on the roads now and stuff like that? Everyone wanted to act cool as if they were not tensed at all.

"Hey guys. What's new?" Suraj wrote on a common wall.

"Nothing dude, just waiting for the results." Suman replied.

"What are you waiting for dude? You know you will pass." I said.

"No man. I don't know. My medicine paper wasn't that great." Suraj said.

"Ohh did you miss out a question? Too bad! Now you'll only rank second." Suman said.

"Whatever man." and Suraj signed off.

"Such a jerk." Suman typed in.

"Forget it man. He deserves the rank. Anyways I thought this time I'll let him have it. Ha-ha." I said with a sense of sarcasm.

"Yeah why not!" Anand replied.

This way the conversation among us friends carried on.

A new window popped up.

"Hi" it was BD, my roommate.

"Hey what's up?" I replied.

"I'm freaking out man." He said.

Why the hell would he freak out? I mean he was sure to pass. He was one of the most decent kids in college, had good terms with all the professors, never had a girlfriend and never got into trouble. And more over he was good at studies. On the other hand I was the guy who never touched his books, was never single, the administration hated me for breaking rules, and I had the maximum number of suspensions. I was glad I wasn't dismissed from the college. And he was freaking out. Jerk!

"If I fail what would I tell my parents? They had put me into MBBS with so much of expectations. If I don't stand up to their expectations they will be so disappointed. What should I do?"

"Relax man, you'll pass. Everyone would." I had my fingers crossed.

Whatever he said made me think. "Would my dad be so disappointed in me? I mean he knows that I'm not that good at studies but is he expecting that much from me? I remember the reason why I joined med school was him but still. Was I a disappointment for him? Was I always one? All the suspensions, declining scores every semester, and even before joining med school, was he happy with his son?"

BD just put me in so much of deep thoughts.

"I was so much different when I had joined this college. We were such kids, all of us. And look at us now. How we have changed haven't we?" Another chat from BD popped in.

I couldn't stop thinking about everything he had said. I was thinking about how much of a disappointment I was for my dad since even before med school. The last four and a half years of my life were flashing back into my head. I couldn't stop remembering.

Chapter Two

"LET US GO BACK IN TIME"

When I passed out of 12th, it was such a relief, mostly because mom and dad wouldn't stop me from doing anything, the reason being my good 84.5% score in board exams. It was supposed to be a pretty good score. I was having the best days of my life, sleeping as long as I wanted, hanging out with friends every day, no more tuition, no more studies. I was so happy!

Dad used to torture me daily about what I wanted to do after this. In the sense which college I wanted to join? And I used to ignore the question every time he would ask me. He used to suggest different colleges, engineering, business school and many more every day. He always used to stress on med school but me being a spoiled kid, refused to think over it. He ended up giving me a dead line of three weeks to think over it and let him know. If I was not to reach a conclusion, mom and dad would decide where I should join. I was fine with it, as I never really cared.

Over the next few days I got more close to the math and commerce section guys, you know the jobless kind. I used to roam around with them all the time, eat outside, and honk at girls, the normal guy stuff. My friendship was improving with Sunny. He was from math section. His house was close by so he would walk up to my house and we would pick up one of my bikes and off we went.

I had recently broken off with my ex-girlfriend, to be more precise my 1st girlfriend, Sushma. We had it going on for almost a year until she left for Delhi after the board results. No letter no message and no phone call. She just left. I wasn't really heartbroken but still wasn't quite ready to get into another relationship until I met Samyukta.

It was because of Sunny that I had met her. He had made this friend Shruti over the phone somehow. And it had been more than a month that they had been chatting. They had finally decided to meet but neither of them was ready to meet alone. They were supposed to bring a friend with them. Sunny chose me and Samyukta was her friend who came along.

He introduced me to both of them and we spoke for some time. It was mostly them talking, Sunny and Shruti. I never knew Sunny could blabber so much. After about an hour we decided to leave. Sunny, that idiot wanted to drive Shruti home. So we switched. He went off with Shruti on her scooty and I was supposed to drop Samyukta home. I drove very decently, very slow, applied brakes very politely, and not very often. I dropped her home and then went to pick up Sunny.

On our way back home I received a text.

"Wana meet up tmrw?"

It was from an unknown number, but I knew who it was. Did she like me? Was she hitting on me? Should I meet her again?

I and Sunny decided to go together. So there we were again, at the same spot the four of us again. We spoke for some time when Shruti whispered something into Samyukta's ears, and suddenly they were fighting for their phones. Somehow she struggled to pass both their phones to me. What was it? What was it that she wanted me to see? I looked into the phone to find out. Shruti wanted me to read the conversation they had through messages last night.

Sam—I had a nice time.

Shruti—Me too, did you like the guys?

Sam—He is cute!

Shruti—I know!

Sam—No not Sunny. I mean he is ok. But Himanshu was really cute. Do you think he is single?

Shraddha—I don't know. You want me to find out?

Sam—I guess. I mean if he is single its good no?

Shraddha—How about you ask him yourself?

This was when I had received the message from Sam if we wanted to meet again. I read the whole conversation. I was smiling or rather blushing. I looked up to find Sunny and Shruti teasing Sam who was blushing her way to glory. She was so red. This was when I knew that I wasn't going to stay single for very long.

On the same day Sunny had asked Shruti out. And we started going for double dates only to part after dinner to drop them home separately. It was funny how a drive to Sam's home took over an hour even though it was at a distance of just 5 minutes. 4 days later she asked me if I wanted to have a girlfriend. It was an indirect proposal. Of course I said yes. We started to spend more time together. Late night calls started. We used to go for long drives every night. Sometimes we used to drive to this dam which was about 20 kilometres from our city. And during these drives applying brakes for no good reason was an often happening. Sometimes she used to drive. Not that she knew how to but teaching her was fun, especially when she would apply brakes.

Three weeks had passed by and I had to make a decision. But I hadn't made any. My aim was only to somehow convince my dad to not make me join med school which he was trying his best to. He had made his elder brother, who was a doctor himself, talk to me and try to convince me. That wasn't it. All his doctor friends had called me and told me how good it would be to be in this profession. I was targeted very well from all directions. My dad had struck me hard enough.

But I had seen my elder brother and sister. Even though they both were doctors now and highly recommended it, I had seen what they had gone through during their course. Raj was always frustrated with the place, ragging, food problem, not being able to manage with the people around. He was a mommy's kid. But my sister, she enjoyed med school. I had seen her cramming like crazy. Once I had seen her reading this book which was the size of all my 12th standard books kept together. I knew if I had to join med school I will be doomed.

And so I was. My explanations weren't good enough to stop him from sending me to med school. He was determined, and frankly neither did I see a better option to make my life worthy enough. I mean I had seen the way his patients treated him, like God. The fame, the respect, everything counted. Inside me I always had this urge to be someone like that. I wasn't ready to sacrifice five full years of my good life in not just studying but not doing anything else. I mean, how many doctors you know who have actually enjoyed their lives in med school?

The decision was taken. But where was the question. There were so many colleges to choose from. Soon I was put in this crash course. So much of physics, chemistry, botany and zoology were in front of me. Who needs to know all that? Even if I had to become a doctor why would I need to know what the botanical name of some plant is, or why a dog is called "Canis familiaris" in zoology?

I had had enough. I was not the kind who would study their ass off. I wasn't going to join med school. I had made my choice. I didn't know what else to do but I wasn't going to go for med school for sure. I had put this idea directly to my dad. Obviously he wasn't happy about it. We argued. For the 1st time mom didn't support me. Instead she tried all the sentimental stuff on me, like they had so much hopes and expectations from me, you know the normal parents crap. But I didn't melt down this time. I stood by my decision. But my dad also stood by his.

A few days passed by and we were supposed to go to Kochi, to check out this med school. My parents wanted to know if the campus would or wouldn't spoil their child. Would he become a doctor there or would he ruin his life? Would he commit suicide after getting ragged?" The normal parent's thoughts!

We reached the airport and found out that the college was about 25 kilometres away.

"How would he travel to the airport? How would he come home so often?" Mom questioned.

The normal motherly tension lightening had struck her. And I was happy it was in my favour.

"Would he even be able to travel alone, how would he manage taxi, how would he manage money?" She continued.

Now it was starting to get annoying. I mean I wasn't that little of a child. Was I??

Dad had little trouble talking to the people over the counter but he managed to hire a taxi. On the way mom and dad had a lot of arguments, surprisingly all favouring me not joining the college. Topics about the weather and climate, the distance from the airport, food problems, staying so far away from home for the first time and many more were discussed. It ended all in favour of me. Now how could dad win against mom? And mom was, for some reason, taking my side this time. I was hoping she wouldn't like the campus either, making my job a little easier, because mom's always win, right?

After a pathetic ride of an hour or so on a very bumpy road, we reached the campus. It was a huge campus. It had tall buildings, like some 10 or 12 stories. I was actually surprised that this part of India was so much developed. We stayed in one of the 16 storied buildings called guest house. It was almost 8 pm by the time we settled down. Dad had got us some parcel from outside. We had our food, if you could call that food. And then off to sleep we went. My bums were woken up again by my dad's foot by around 8 am. It was annoying but did I have an option? We were supposed to meet the manager at 10 am. We reached in time when our number was called. He told us all about the college, how good it was, how students were taken care of so well and how ragging was never an issue. Mom and dad believed him as if he was going to say something bad about the college.

We were then supposed to meet Dr.C.G.Nayar. She was the chief warden. Her office was on the 6th floor. We decided to take the elevator. Where we found out that the elevators were separate for the guys and girls. Now that was so stupid. I know a lot can happen with in an elevator but which idiot would try to do something during college time? I had begun to realize how stupid the college was.

As soon as we entered her office, she greeted us very well. We sat down and they discussed the basic stuff again, ragging, hostel, food etc.

"He is like my own child, we all live here as a family. I promise I would take care of him as my own family."

All of a sudden I had another mom, such a bitch. I knew she would have said the same dialogue to everyone who came to meet her.

We had a tour of the whole campus, the college as well the hospital. Soon we finished all the formalities and filled all the forms. Everything was done and finally we could go back. We had our flight the next morning so we decided to go to the city. We were surprised to find out that the city was about 10 kilometres from the college, another reason for me to not join the college. Farther the city, lesser the fun and lesser the girls, I was determined not to join the college.

We were home by noon, and the first thing I did as soon as I reached home was to call Sam and arrange a meet up. Yes I had missed her. In less than half an hour I was all refreshed ready to leave.

"Where do you think you are going" mom asked.

"Nowhere maa, just to meet friends. Find out what I missed out in these days."

She seemed fine with it. Dad was also there but he didn't utter a word. I failed to understand what was going through his mind. But at that point of time it really didn't matter to me. I was back in my home town, the place I loved, the place I was supposed to be, with friends. My life was here, and I was happy here.

I met Sam. She was angry with me as I hadn't told her that I was going to be away for few days. I only realized that it got her angrier when I told her that my parents had decided to put me into this college far far away from my city. She was angry at first, but then realized that it wouldn't work out. Long distances relationships never work out you know. She got emotional, normal oestrogen effect. She tried breaking up with me right then but I held on. That was when I decided that I'll tell my dad that I wouldn't go so far away for med school. Not that Sam was the real reason. I never really wanted to go so far away from home. I was scared of loneliness, of responsibilities, of studies; I was scared of growing up. I never wanted to go. But I couldn't have explained these reasons to my heart. I had to grow up. But Sam was one reason that my heart would understand. And so I decided to stand up for it.

That evening I went home all bold and strong determined to tell dad that I wasn't going to go so far away. Mom and dad were sitting in the hall discussing something. Suddenly there was silence the second I walked in.

Maybe it was the attitude I had on me at that time. I went up straight up to my dad and said.

"I'm never going to go to that college, so far away. Actually, I'm not going to join med school at all!"

"So what will you do?" He asked.

"I don't know." I replied.

"So you won't join MBBS?" He asked angrily.

I was about to say no when something very strong hit me on my cheeks. It was dad. He had slapped me. I couldn't believe it. For the first time in my life he had hit me. Not that I was thinking to rebel back, but I was still angry and determined with what I had decided. I started walking away towards my room and on the way screamed and threatened my dad.

"If you force me to go to that college, I swear I will run away from there." I threatened him.

"Don't you walk away from me like that, come back here." My dad screamed.

I only ignored him to bang the door of my room.

I had disrespected my father. I was feeling guilty. But I couldn't go and apologize to him. If I did, that would mean that I would have to agree to go to the college as well. I didn't know what to do. But he was my father, how could I do this? I hated myself. I had to bow down in front of him. After all whatever he wants me to do will be for my own good, right?

I went out in the hall again. Mom and dad were still sitting there, and as expected silence occurred as soon as I entered the hall. I went and sat close to my dad. Words were not coming out of my mouth. I didn't know what to do. I somehow gather the strength to say—"I'm sorry dad."

He immediately got up and left the hall. He had not forgiven me. Mom got up, kept her palm over my cheeks for a second and then left. I was lonely. I didn't have any shoulder to cry on. I didn't have anyone to hug. I sat there alone and cried. Partly for the stupid mistake I had done, and partly for the fact that my life was definitely going to be doomed in that college.

Chapter Three

"LOSING MY INDEPENDENCE"

I still remember it was the evening of 15th August 2005 when mom and dad had left me in the hostel. For the whole nation it was the Independence Day, but I was crying over losing mine. I was going to be trapped here for the next five years.

When we reached the hostel, the warden greeted us. I'm guessing he was really trying hard to smile, but by his expression it looked like he was saying "Welcome to hell, your life is now doomed, ha-ha." He was a baldy who looked like the guys who hang people in jails, only a thinner version, very thin. He blabbered something in Malayalam and then told me that my room was on the third floor. Mom and dad waited in the guest room while the ultra-thin warden led my way to my room.

As soon as I entered my room I was shocked. My bathroom back at home was bigger than this room. And moreover I had to share this room with another person. How was I supposed to manage in here? I had never shared a single thing in my life, and all of a sudden I was dumped in this place. I was never so upset. My roommate had gone out. His name was Brahma Dutt. It looked like he was from some ancient era. I mean who has those kinds of names any more. I didn't know how I would manage to be with him. I was supposed to spend the next five years with him, in the sense share the room with him. How was I going to manage that?

I went down again to see off my parents, the devils who had left me in this hell, to die alone. They had a flight to catch so they left soon enough. They told the normal parent stuff before they left.

"Be a nice kid. Don't get into trouble. And if you have any kind of a problem, you know you can always count on us."

But I also knew how they would react if I had to call them up and put forward a problem, you know how normal parents would react. "Grow up son. It's high time you realize your responsibilities and stand up for it yourselves. You can't depend on us forever. Can you?"

I ran back to my room, closed the door, lay down on my bed, which was as hard as a rock and cried and cried to stop only when my roommate came back. I had to stop crying. I had to act cool or if not, at least not look so weak and terrible.

I opened the door to find this guy, rather a kid with a not really required moustache. He looked innocent, you know the kind of dumb roommate you would want to have. He greeted me in a decent way and I responded accordingly, not that we were going to jump up and hug each other as we had known each other for years or something. He came in, changed to his night clothes and was ready to walk out again. There was a lot of noise outside in the corridor. All the guys were mingling up in the normal boy's way, making lot of noise.

"You are coming? BD asked.

"Where?" I enquired.

"Don't you want to get to know your new batch mates?" BD asked again.

"May be sometime later." I replied.

"Tensed?" Another question came from BD.

"About what?" I asked again.

"You know, new college, far from home, new people around, MBBS?" He said in a calm voice.

All of a sudden this kid became like this elder brother who knew everything. He was taking his steps back to his bed. I thought he was going to stay and support me, but I wasn't really ready for that. I was about to burst out in tears again and I didn't want him around.

"No. I'm fine. You go on, meet them. I'll see them in class any ways." I said.

"Are you sure?" He insisted.

"Yes. Go on now." I concluded.

He closed the door behind him and I was on my bed crying my eyes out again.

Sleeping that night was a little difficult. I kept thinking about how messed up my life was going to be, how was I going to manage in this hell hole? All I could think of, was to go home, or at least be with someone who I knew, Sam, Sunny, my school friends, anyone would be fine. But all those days were history. I was never going to get those days back. In the middle of these thoughts I slowly drifted away to sleep after 3 am.

I was disturbed by a lot of noise early in the morning. My roommate himself was yelling out my name.

"Himanshu, get up. You are getting late." BD screamed.

"Class is supposed to be only at 8." I said in a cranky voice.

"What time do you think it is already?" He said sarcastically.

I got up to check my watch. "Fuck its 7.40 am already, couldn't you wake me up earlier?"

Yelling this out loud I made my run to the common bathroom which was another fucking stupid thing about that place.

I was back in less than ten minutes. BD was ready but he was waiting for me. "2 minutes" I said gesturing with my fingers.

We left for the class together. College was about 10 minutes' walk from the hostel. We covered that distance in less than 4 minutes on our running feet and reached the side of boy's elevator.

"The lecture halls are on the 11th floor!" One of the students exclaimed.

We all realized that we were never going to make it in time. Both the lifts were going up, one on the 4th floor and the other on the 6th. By the time they came back and took us up, it would definitely be past 8. 1st day, 1st class, and we were late. Couldn't we ask for anything better?

I grabbed BD's hand and walked towards the stairs.

"Are you crazy? I'm not going to climb up eleven stairs!" He reacted.

"Dude just shut up and follow me." I ordered.

We went up to the first floor, the front and back of the building was connected through the pathology dept on the first floor. Using the girls lift was my idea. Usually girls are on time, they would have reached the class at least by 7.30 am. And my guess was also right. When the lift opened, there were only four girls inside, with one old man who looked like a professor. We wished him and got inside the lift. During the time in the lift, BD kept whispering things like "if I get into trouble I'm telling that it was your idea" and "I don't want to get into trouble on my 1st day of college" and I would just calm him down somehow. The old man dropped down at 4th floor which was the administration floor. And the lift kept rising after that. We kept wondering who that could have been. But we didn't have much time. As soon as the lift reached the top and the doors opened, we ran up to the lecture hall. The door was closed. The other guys were probably still waiting for the lift on the other side because there was no sign of them. The door was half made of glass so we could peep inside. I was the first one to do that and Aditya who was sitting on the first bench gestured to me not to get in. But me being an idiot, I knocked on the door and got in.

"May I come in sir?" I asked.

The professor turned around to say "You may not!"

Apparently he had just given a small lecture on how much he hates late comers. That explained why Aditya was trying to stop me.

He looked like the older brother of my warden, the only difference was that this guy had a clean shave and was wearing a white apron. His name was Dr. Sebastian and he was a professor of physiology.

"What do you think of yourself gentleman? It's the first day of college and you couldn't even make it on time. Now that makes me wonder how you are going to perform for the rest of the year."

BD and the other girls were standing behind me, all of us listening to whatever crap he had to say. He continued his lecture for another 5 min, blaming me again for wasting that much time during which he could have actually taught us something. And then he let us enter the class. We had to sit in the front rows because they were the only ones that were empty. As soon as we sat on our places, the rest of the boys who had been waiting for the lift on the other side showed up at the door and we heard another long lecture about latecomers and how they should be treated.

He was taking class on action potential, about how current passes through your muscles every time you do something. Now would you have ever known that when you are putting something in your mouth, a stream of current starts from the base of your good for nothing brain, travels through your spinal cord and then reaches the muscles via the peripheral nerves, which make your hand move towards your mouth. Once again when you put your food into your mouth, the taste buds on your tongue get the perception and through nerves send it to your brains where you understand the taste of the food. Now tell me frankly, would you ever think of all this when you are eating something.

We somehow managed to sit through his class of utter non sense and were only waiting for the time he would finish. Soon enough he was done with his lecture. While opening the attendance register he kept blaming us for wasting his time. As soon as he left the hall we were about to get up and run for the back benches. But before we could even get up this short, kind of funny looking lady walked in. She was dark, had a mix of black and white hair, and that was the only thing that didn't match with the rest of her. Looking at her the 1st thing that clicked my mind was the song "blue da ba dee". It was like a blue day for her. Her saree was a shade of blue, with blue ear rings and a pendent which was also blue, blue bangles, even her ring was blue. Her shoes had a blue flower on them and to complete the picture she was carrying a blue file in her hands. We could only wonder what this blue clown was going to teach us.

She turned out to be the HOD of anatomy, and she gave a very good competition to Dr Sebastian to how useless things you could talk about. She was teaching us embryology, how the face of a baby was formed inside the uterus, how at first the baby is a, you know in the middle, and only later the baby becomes a boy or a girl. Usually people don't really care about what goes inside there, do we? Once the baby is out, that is when we start caring, till then we just take care only of the mother. So why was she teaching us all this crap?

It was a huge relief when she got done with her class. As expected she took attendance, and then left.

Next we were supposed to go to the anatomy dissection hall. This was where all the dead bodies were cut open with the intention of teaching us the basic anatomy of a human body. I thought cutting open a dead body would be fun. As soon as we reached the dissection hall we saw the whole crowd on one side of the hall. They were looking for something on the notice board. It was the distribution of students among the dissection tables. There were six tables with one dead body on them each and students were equally distributed among them.

We were just settling down on out tables when the same guy who we met in the lift earlier walked into the dissection hall with his eyes wandering all over as if they were searching for someone. His eyes took a pause on BD's tables and then after sometime halted on mine. After that he had some discussion with the teachers sitting on the staff table. In a few more seconds mine and BD's name were called out.

"Brahma Dutt and Himanshu Patel are required at the principal's office immediately." Dr. Prashant, an anatomy professor announced.

I and BD had an eye contact and it was evident that he wanted to kill me.

We walked down to the 4th floor, where the principal's office was. His secretary asked us to wait. After about five minutes we were called in.

"Isn't this your first day?" He asked.

"Yes sir!" We replied in chorus.

"So is it that both of you like getting into trouble or breaking rules seems like an adventure?" He asked again.

"I didn't get you sir?" I enquired.

"Are you fond of using the lift allotted only for females, which males are not allowed to use?" He questioned further.

"If that was the case then why is it that he was in that lift as well? Wasn't he man enough?" This thought crossed my mind.

"But sir . . ." I had just started to speak when BD spoke.

"We are sorry sir. This mistake wouldn't be repeated again. We sincerely apologize." BD apologized interrupting me.

"Don't think that I have forgiven you. From now on I will personally keep an eye over both of you. Be careful, you don't want to spend the rest of your life in this college do you?" He questioned again staring at us.

We both denied.

"Very well then, you can go back to your class." He declared.

On the way back I and BD had an argument.

"Why didn't you let me speak?" I asked.

"Why should I have, so that you could have messed up the situation even more?" He responded in anger.

"That was a stupid thing to be caught for, using the female's lift. That is so dumb, where in the whole world would anyone do this? Divide lifts for boys and girls." I asked out of my frustration.

"That's not the point Himanshu. I have a friend who has passed out from this college. He told me that even the most stupid mistakes you would do can make your course extend by one or even two years. That's why I didn't want you to speak because it wouldn't have been a good idea to argue with the principal. Moreover I want to get out of this college as soon as possible" BD tried to explain.

"So do I man. It's just the first day and I hate this place already." I confessed.

"Now let's rush to the dissection hall. I don't want to miss cutting open the dead bodies." BD said.

At this point we were standing in front of the girls lift, which had just opened up. We both looked at each other.

"What do you say?" I asked BD.

"No way man." He said with a scared look on his face.

And within seconds I convinced him to use the lift once more, because the principal was in his office and there were no girls in the lift. It was empty.

Maybe I wasn't lucky enough or maybe BD was very unlucky, the doors of the elevator opened up on the 6th floor where an old lady, probably in her early 50's walked in. I recognized her immediately. It was Dr. C.G. Nayar.

"Are you first year students?" She enquired.

"Yes ma'am." We replied.

"Don't you know that you're not supposed to use these lifts?" She asked with her face getting red.

"But ma'am we were getting late for class." I gave the excuse.

"Whose fault is that, mine or yours?" She asked.

"We are sorry ma'am." BD said and I joined him to say "we won't repeat this again ma'am."

"I'm leaving you because it's your first time, but don't repeat this again. Ok?" The redness of her cheeks reduced.

"Yes ma'am." We replied in chorus.

The lift had reached the 10 floor. She was going up to the 11th floor to take lectures. And luckily we were not late for cutting open the dead bodies.

     The day was not even half way through and I had broken a rule, twice already. As soon as we entered the dissection hall I was called by Dr Prashant, the same old professor who announced our names.

"Who do you think you are? What is this that you are wearing?" he asked me.

As we had not received our uniforms and aprons yet, yes we have uniforms, we could wear casual clothes to college for the time being. I was wearing blue jeans with a black t-shirt which had some crazy skull design. For some reason I had not understood the question and thanks to my great sense of humour I replied "Jeans and a T-shirt sir."

"So now your acting over smart also huh? This won't work here. You can't wear jeans and other clothes like this."

Then he turned towards the crowd to speak louder "No jeans and designer clothes are allowed in the dissection hall. This is a class room not a fashion show ramp. People who don't come dressed properly will be thrown out of the class." and then he looked at me.

Till now I had learned something from BD and even though it was a little difficult but I managed to say "I'm sorry sir. I will try not to repeat this again."

He didn't say anything else but turned and walked away.

We walked back to our dissection tables and took our seats waiting for our table teacher to come.

We had fun doing the dissection. Mostly I was the one enjoying. My dad being a surgeon, I had had the opportunities to sneak into his operation theatres to see his surgeries, so I wasn't really grossed out when I saw the dead bodies. It was even more fun because of our table teacher Dr. Susy. She was this slim tall female, who didn't even know how to walk properly, but was good enough to have a teacher crush on, especially when compared with those beautiful girls we had as our batch mates. The reason why we enjoyed Susy ma'am was because she wouldn't know what she was talking.

"And students, this is the radial nerve, wait. Is it? It looks like it is. Maybe it is the ulnar nerve. No no, this is the ulnar nerve and that is the radial nerve."

While we would try to take a peek in and realize what she was holding with her forceps she would speak again or rather confuse us more.

"No no. The first one which I was holding, yes this one. This is the radial nerve. I hope it is. Anyways moving on to the next structure, muscles of the hand. This one looks like the . . ." and she would continue with the class and her mind overflowing with confidence.

It was good in one way. For the fact that we would get so confused that we would come back and read ourselves and then go back and tell her which one was radial and ulnar nerve. At least she made us study right.

This way the dissection went on for another hour or so. In the dissection hall from where everyone was sitting everyone could have a view of the rest of the students. This was helpful for us boys to check out the girls during attendance time. I and Roshan, would sit next to each other and our conversations would go something like this.

"Hey that one is really cute."

"But she is too thin."

"But she has stuff at the right places man."

"No dude, there are better ones."

"Ok fine. What about that one?"

And our conversations would go on.

As soon as the dissection was over, we had an hour for lunch break. It was a relief for once we had time to wait for the lifts on the boy's side and BD was happy that I wasn't running towards trouble again. The mess hall was on the 5th floor of the hospital building. As we reached the ground floor of the hospital building we realized that the lifts were filled with boys and girls, together. But BD didn't want to risk it again and so he took the stairs. And guess who he forced to come with him, yes me!

Climbing five floors was tiring and it made us hungrier. We entered the mess which was very noisy and crowded, as if it was some famous restaurant. We washed our hands and joined the line. After about ten minutes we reached the food containers. The first two had pickles which I skipped. The next two had rice, one was white rice and the other was parboiled one. After that there was this yellow looking curry which was made of god knows what, followed by cabbage curry, curd and pappad. Now what was annoying here was that we could take as much of the yellow shit we wanted but they would give us only one small bowl of curd and 2 pappads.

With our first bites we realized why everyone usually complains of their college's mess. It was evident that the food royally sucked. We somehow managed to stuff ourselves as we had no other option. Or at least we didn't know of the options on the first day of college.

Next we had physiology practical, where we met the biggest bitch of our 1st year among the teachers. Dr. Veena was taking our first practical class. We were divided into 4 batches, A, B, C and D, of 25 students each. And not to our surprise we had no good looking girls in our batch. Boys are never lucky for these kinds of things you know, especially the ones who are expecting a lot.

The class was on WBC count. She taught us how to do the steps properly and then she asked for a volunteer. I being the smarter one stepped forward. It was a stupid thing to do as I didn't even know why she wanted a volunteer.

"Give me your hand." she commanded.

"Aaahhhh" even before I could have realized what was going to happen she had grabbed my index finger and poked it deep with a lancet. I tried to retrieve my hand but she was holding it tight. A drop or two of blood oozed out of my finger and I had no idea what she was trying to do. She turned my finger towards a glass slide and dropped my blood over it. Then she did some crazy shit and said.

"This is how you prepare your slides and then observe under microscope ok. Now all of you prepare your slides and then I will teach you what to look for in the slides. Now go to your allotted places."

I was happy that at least I won't have to poke myself again. I moved forward to take the slide she had made out of my blood. As I was about to reach it, she slapped hard on my hand saying:

"Go and make your own slide again." She said with an evil smile.

It was my blood she had used. Now what was I supposed to do, poke myself again. But why? Now imagine, if I had to become this famous neurosurgeon or a cardiologist, will I be poking myself to see what's in it? No man. The lab technicians or sisters are supposed to do that. Then why the hell are we supposed to do this crazy shit? I was pissed.

She then taught us the rest of the practical shit and we followed her and did our records. Once we got it signed by her we could go back. I had to poke myself three times to get more blood because I screwed up the initial slides but in the end I made it. That was some achievement, especially for the first day.

We took the stairs all the way down from the 8th floor, then walked straight back to the hostel and fell asleep. College was tiring after all. Now who are all those crazy people who say college is fun? I don't think so.

We spent the next few hours in different rooms, trying to get to know each other. I met many new people. Realized some were born jerks. The rest I could rely on. It was fun knowing getting to know the new people, or new friends I'd rather call them.

Chapter Four

"UNHEALTHY INTERACTION"

Soon it was 7.30 pm, time for dinner. You never know when time flies when you are talking, especially when you are talking shit, with people you don't know or you are trying to know. Because you are trying to find out if he is a bigger jerk than yourself. And you don't stop until you somehow convince yourself that you are better than the other person.

We all went to the mess hall. We had all expected to see our seniors sometime soon and the mess was the best place to meet them. This was the first sight of seniors, the whole bunch of them. Though we were told that there is no ragging in this institution but we had brains. Most of us were scared; maybe that's why most of us had decided to walk in groups.

We joined the line as usual. Somehow I was pushed up all the way to the front just behind a senior. The line was slowly moving forward towards the food. Suddenly I got a push from the back and I hit the senior in front of me. He turned around to stare at me. I was scared, not just because he was my senior, but more because he was this huge dark fat guy at least 4 inches taller than me. For some reason I knew I was going to be the first one amongst my batch mates to be ragged and I knew it was going to happen soon enough.

After taking food in our plates we took the tables on far corners of the hall, as far as possible from the senior's table. The food was good, as in better than the shit we had in the afternoon. But for obvious reasons I was not able to eat properly. It had just been a day in this new place, far from mom and dad, home sickness and then the fear of this huge senior who was ready to rag me where ever he would find me.

We finished having our food, washed our plates and we were chatting our way up to the third floor. I could hear my new friends talking crap but I had not joined in this time. I had something bigger to worry about, that senior. And there he was standing on the third floor balcony waiting for me. As soon as I saw him I tried to hide myself behind Arvind. He could not hide me as he was a little shorter and thinner than me and the senior saw me. I knew I was going to be dead. He was going to rag me and remembering all the stories I had heard from my other friends from engineering and business colleges, I was shitting in my pants already.

He showed his hand in a way I understood he was calling me. I started walking towards him and all my new friends who I was thinking to rely on had started walking away from me, those idiots.

"What's your name??" He asked in a heavy voice.

"Himanshu" I squeaked.

"Don't you have a father?" His voice got heavier.

"Yes I do!" I squeaked again.

"So say your full name." He almost screamed.

"Himanshu R Patel." I replied in a low tone.

"Where are you from?" He continued questioning.

"Raipur" I replied.

"Where?" With a surprised expression he asked.

Now what was I supposed to say. If he didn't know the city from which I was from then what am I supposed to tell him.

"Say the full name of the place." He screamed.

I didn't get the question but my stupid brain made me answer this "KIMS Hospital, Agrasen square, Raipur, Chattisgarh, India."

He came closer to my face and said "Listen; don't try to act cool in front of me ok. You are just a fresher. You don't want your seniors to hate you and then not help you later on for your exams. Be careful buddy. You are going to need us and so you better get rid of your shitty attitude. Get it?"

"Yes Sir." I replied.

"Do I have white hair?" He questioned.

"No." I replied with a doubtful thought.

"Do I look like I have no sense of clothing?" He questioned.

"No." I replied.

"Do I look like I'm talking non sense?" Now he was getting annoyed.

"Yes!"

That's what I wanted to say but I denied that also.

"Then why are you calling me a sir? Do I look like those professors in the lecture halls?" His eyes were now red.

"No Sir. I mean what am I supposed to call you then?" I asked with a lot of courage.

"Are you asking me a question?" He said with a smirk.

"Yes." I replied boldly.

"You are not supposed to. Do you even know my name?" He asked.

"No Sir." Now I was getting annoyed.

"Stop calling me Sir!" He ordered.

"Ok Sir." I replied.

"What is my name?" He questioned again.

"I don't know." I said shrugging my shoulders.

"So that is your assignment for today. Find out my name, but don't bother asking any of my batch mates because they are not going to tell you. Ok?" He said preparing himself to leave.

"Ok Sir." I took a sigh.

"And stop calling me sir."

With his last line he was walking away from me. On my way back to my room I was thinking how I was supposed to find his name, without even asking anyone else. One thing was for sure; I was going to call him sir until he would get frustrated and tell me what I'm supposed to call him. I was hoping it would work.

So was that it, my name, my place and an advice? Was that all? I thought ragging was much more than that. At least I was happy for the fact that my ragging session was done.

As I got back to my room I found this huge bunch of people in my room, the newly made friends, and the same people who abandoned me on the very sight of the senior, and now they were here to find out how I was after my ragging. Jerks!

I told them the whole story, my name and address and me acting cool and calling him sir, everything. We all had actually started to think that this place was truly an institution where there was no ragging. But our hopes were shattered soon.

Someone was knocking at the door, to be more precise that person was banging at the door. My roommate opened the door and two guys walked in. They were definitely not from my batch and that could mean only one thing. SENIORS!

Which one of you is Himanshu? One of them asked.

No one moved. Not even me.

"Do you all want to get ragged or . . ." The other one had just started when three of my friends were pointing at me already.

"Come out, now!" Both of them ordered.

I walked out only hoping I wouldn't end up in the hospital after the ragging session. I followed them till the end of the corridor where there was a bigger group of people, about ten of them. For a second I thought it was more of my batch mates who were going to get ragged by few seniors. But none of their faces looked familiar.

It took me only a split second to realize that I was definitely going to end up in the hospital after this session. The reason why the faces were not familiar was because none of them were my batch mates. They were all my seniors, more than ten of them. And I had no idea what I was going to do. I was going to get killed right there and I could do nothing about it.

"So Mr. Himanshu, do you want to tell me your name?" The apparent leader of the gang asked.

"Himanshu R Patel!" I responded with my experience.

Hmmm you are getting better already. So I have heard that you have a lot of attitude. Is it so? He enquired.

I kept quiet.

"Would you mind answering my question Himanshu sir?" He taunted me.

"Yes sir. I mean no sir. I don't have attitude sir." I answered.

"Would you stop calling me sir? I'm not your teacher." He said annoyingly.

"Yes sir. I mean Yes!" I replied with hesitation. I was sure the sir thing was not going to work out in front of ten seniors, so I surrendered.

"Ok so you know what this is right?" He questioned with a smile.

I didn't even move my lips. I had no idea what to say.

"I'm waiting for an answer Himanshu!" He said getting angry.

"Ragging?" I replied in an uncomfortable voice.

"So you think this is ragging? Is it so my friends." And all those ten devils started laughing.

"Himanshu, this isn't ragging. This is called a healthy interaction ok." Gesturing with his finger he said.

It was a healthy interaction in what way, healthy for whom, for their laughing muscles? How could anyone be so ruthless, so cruel, ragging someone, ten of them, and me alone, just one small kid? I was almost about to cry out loud.

"Ok we'll make this quick ok. Then you can go back to your room." He said clapping his hands together.

I had no idea what he meant. I had recently seen the movie Shaw Shank Redemption and all that I could think of was the scene from that movie where a bunch of people surround the actor and then, you know, take advantage of him. What was I supposed to do? Retaliate? Rebel or just let them have me, take advantage of me? May be this is the way it happens in college. May be everyone has to go through this. May be, but I didn't want to. Oh god, help me please.

"What is this?" He asked holding a banana in his hand.

Oh my god. Now he was going to use a banana or what?

"It looks like a banana to me sir." I replied.

"Ok. So it is a banana. What do you think it can be used for?" He asked.

"To eat sir." I replied.

"Do you think I don't have brains? Don't you think I don't know that banana is a fruit meant to be eaten?" He asked forming a fist with his right hand.

"So why the fuck are you asking me? Leave me alone. Can't you see I don't want to get ragged by you homosexual seniors." is what I wanted to say but I ended up apologizing to him.

"What are the other uses of a banana?" Another senior stepped forward and asked.

What was I going to answer to that? He wouldn't even let me talk properly. And now he wanted me to tell him the different uses of a banana. And so obviously I didn't say anything.

"So you don't know." He queried.

"I don't think so." I replied.

"Say yes or no. You don't have to pour your attitude in your words ok." A third senior said getting closer to me.

"No." In a scared tone I answered.

"At least tell me the gender which uses it more often." The leader asked.

"I don't know." I replied.

"Boys or girls? Come on man. At least answer that." He asked with a smile.

"Girls." I said looking down expecting another embarrassing question.

"So you think girls use bananas more than boys. In what way do you think they use it more than guys?" There came my embarrassing question.

I kept my mouth shut. But behind me I could hear all those seniors laughing at me like I was dropadi and that senior ragging me was duryodhan raping me in front of the seniors who were laughing at me just like the court men of dhrithrashtra.

After a little while he decided to let go of that topic. Instead he decided to hit me with something else.

"What is my name?" He asked.

"I don't know." I replied.

"So go and find out." He said gesturing his finger away from me.

At this point of time I took the most literal meaning of the sentence and started walking away.

"Hello? Where do you think you are going?" He said almost grabbing my shirt from behind.

"I thought you asked me to go and find out your name. So I thought . . ."

"Stop thinking!" He interrupted me.

"This is Karan, Subramanayam, Kiran, Narayan, Arun, Mohammad, Ankit, Sijith, Karan and Himanshu."

And all I could think of was dog, pig, donkey, horse and so on.

"So can you repeat it now?" He asked after introducing all the ten members of the healthy interaction team.

And so I repeated. "Karan, Subramanayam, Kiran, Narayan, Arun, Mohammad, Ankit, Sijith, Karan and Himanshu."

"So you are going to call your seniors by their names but add no suffixes. You have no respect for your seniors. Do you?" He had now started to annoy me.

"It's not like that. I was just . . ."

"Don't give me any excuses!" He said interrupting me.

"But I . . ."

"Stop whining like a pussy." He interrupted me yet again.

This time I decided to shut up.

"Guys anything else or is it enough for this kid today? What do you say? Should we call the next one?" He turned to his gang and asked.

Few of them were like angels who wanted me to go. And call the next victim. But few others wanted him to continue my vastraharan.

"I think it's enough for one day. So did you just get ragged by your seniors?" He turned back to me and asked.

"I think it was just a healthy interaction." I replied with a small smile.

"Good. Now go back to your room and send your room mate here." He ordered me.

"Ok!" I turned around and then remembered something.

"Excuse me. Could I go to the bathroom first and then call him. Please?"

"Is it urgent? Can't you hold a little longer?" He asked with a raised eyebrow.

"I think I can" I replied with a dumb face.

"Then hold it. Now send him here, fast!" He said pointing his finger away from me.

"Ok!" And I was on my way back to my room.

As soon as I entered my corridor, I was shocked. But soon my shock turned into happiness and I couldn't stop smiling. I realized that there was at least one senior in every room and that I was not the only one who got ragged that night. The corridor looked more like those small houses of the village in the movie sholay where gabbar's daaku's were looting the villagers, dragging them out and beating them, that's how I pictured it. My room was towards the other end of the corridor. As I was walking towards my room I could hear a lot of weird things. I heard few people singing the national anthem and a few struggling to remember it and someone yelling their throats out with curses. Another batch mate of mine was holding a mirror in front of him and cursing himself. Few others were doing some kind of acrobatics.

Suddenly Suman came out of his room and started running towards me. I moved out of his way but I kept my eye on him. He ran all the way to the end of the corridor and then ran back to his room. I realized that it would be a part of a healthy interaction as well.

Finally I reached my room. As I entered I realized that my roommate was no exception either. He looked like he was trying to sit on a chair which wasn't there. There was another senior in my room. I was scared but I had stepped inside the room already and couldn't back out any more.

I also realised that if I tell BD to go to those seniors then this one right here in my room would have no one to rag and me being the only victim in the vicinity, he would rag me. So I decided to just keep my mouth shut.

"What's your name?" The senior asked.

"Himanshu R Patel."

"See that's how you should introduce yourself, understand?" He told BD.

"Do you know Malayalam?" He asked me.

I denied.

"Do you know Hindi?" He asked BD.

He denied.

"Ok then. Start cursing each other." He said resting back on the bed.

We both kept quiet.

"Will you guys start or should I?" He said almost ready to curse us.

And I shot the first one. "*****"

BD followed me. "***"

We were yelling out really loud. And in a few moments we could see few heads peeping into our rooms.

I would say something.

And then BD would say something better than that, actually worse.

And then I would say something which would get him angrier and so it went on.

After few minutes of our aggressive word fight, we were interrupted by another senior, one from Drithrashtra's court.

"Where is Himanshu? Yes. Didn't we ask you to send your roommate? Where is he?" He enquired.

And I pointed out towards my roommate.

"You come with me. And Himanshu I think you should come with him too. You didn't send him in time did you?" He said looking at me.

"Why god, why me? Didn't I get into enough trouble in college on the first day that you send these seniors now?" I said to myself.

The senior left us commanding to reach the ragging spot, or rather the healthy interaction class, and gave us few seconds to think of an escape plan. But unfortunately neither I nor BD could think of a good enough excuse for not reporting in time. Blaming it on the other senior who was ragging BD when I entered the room was a bad idea because that would become just another topic to rag us even more. Confused in our own thoughts trying to predict what worse could happen, both of us reported to the group of seniors.

"So Himanshu has already started disobeying seniors? Is it not Himanshu?" The same leader asked me again.

"No, we were about to . . ."

"No excuses. I've heard they call you BD. Would you mind introducing yourself?" He turned towards BD and asked.

BD underwent the normal introduction session. And then came the main part, the healthy part of the interaction.

"I'm tired already. Himanshu would you do me a favour?" He asked me.

I nodded my head in agreement.

"Can you rag BD for me?" He asked.

What the hell, I couldn't even stand there properly and he was asking me to rag him, my roommate, the only person I had got to know in this college so far. I thought over it for a second. And I asked him to hold his ears and do 15 sit ups and surprisingly BD quietly followed my orders. The senior was smiling and so had I started enjoying it.

"10 push ups!" and BD somehow managed to do 7 and gave up. Then I made him run up and down the corridor twice. I was enjoying it. Now I knew why seniors are so keen to rag juniors. When BD came back he was panting already. This was when the senior spoke.

"Himanshu you've got 2 minutes."

I had a question mark on my face.

"You just made your roommate workout. Wouldn't you give him company? Come on now, what were the numbers? 15 sit ups, 10 push ups and then up and down the corridor twice. On your mark, get set, GO!" He almost screamed in excitement.

As I had started doing the sit-ups I could see a bud of laughter growing on BD's face. But he knew as well that if he laughed out loud he would get worse. By the time I came back after my run from the end of the corridor BD was struggling to point out the uses of a banana.

"So you can't think of any other use of a banana?" BD denied.

"No." BD denied.

"Do you know what masturbation is?" The senior continued the healthy interaction.

BD nodded yes.

"How many times do you do it?" He asked.

Obviously BD was quite on that. And I knew I was going to be asked that question. And obviously I kept quite as well.

After a smirk the senior spoke. "Both of you will have an assignment for tomorrow. How many girls are there in your batch?"

"Around 60" I replied.

"I want names of all the girls written on a paper, with their age, address, and hobbies. And you should also rate them out of 10 on how good they look. Ok?"

Yes we rhymed in chorus.

"Go on now. It's late already. We need to sleep as well." The senior dispersed with his gang.

We both started walking away from the dispersing crowd of healthy interacters. On the way we had discussions about how to get the list of girls. We decided that he would do the first half of the batch and I would do the rest. Getting their names and rating them on 10 would have been really easy but then how were we supposed to get their hobbies.

As we reached the room we did realize that it was very late and BD had no intentions of being forced to use the girls lift again the next day. So we both went to sleep and then I got up a few seconds later realizing I had to pee!

Chapter Five

"MY CODE OF MISCONDUCT"

It wasn't that bad of a day, except for the fact that I was caught twice by the principal and C.G. Nayar and then the lecture by Dr Sebastian and Dr Prashant and then getting poked by Dr. Veena, and then the healthy interactions. Other than these things the day had been ok. I had even forgotten that I was away from home. Samyukta never crossed my thoughts. Neither did any of my friends from back home. I had done well for staying away from home the first time. I was happy for I had survived the first day at college.

The next few days at college were like the first one, encounters with new teachers every day, new kind of crazy stuff and new subjects, new practical, new friends, new rules and of course newer ways of homosexual ragging, oops, healthy interactions. It was a new way of living, new responsibilities; life was changing as we all knew it. But one thing hadn't changed. I and Sam both were holding on to each other strong enough. Surprisingly I had actually started to challenge people who thought long distance relations never work out to come and take a look at mine. We were going on well. We spoke every day, had late night talks. In the beginning she used to call the hostel but by the end of 1st week I bought a mobile for myself without even letting my parents know. I was scared about keeping the phone because mobile phones were not allowed. But then I had to talk to her. So I was ready to take the risk.

Even though I was managing with the new friends very well, I still hated the fact that my parents dumped me so far away from home. I had never been so far away from home, that too alone. I had told my father that I was going to run away from here and I had already started making plans so as to how. The college was going to give us six days off on the occasion of onam and I had taken an extra three days leave. My plan was to spend the extra three days in Nagpur with Sam and then go home making it look like I never did a thing wrong. So I took off from the hostel three days before the holidays and reached Nagpur the next day. I wanted to spend at least two days with Sam and have as much fun as possible.

And so I did. Sam was standing there, at the airport, as beautiful as she was, in a white skirt and a black t shirt, looking as cute as possible. And the 1st thing she did was to hug me so tight that I had to push her back to take a breath. The hug was followed by a kiss, yes on the lips, yes in the airport, and yes in the middle of the crowd, amongst all the old and young people. Though embarrassing, I loved it.

Soon we were off to her apartment. She lived alone in a flat. It was a little difficult to compromise about her living alone, you know, long distance, far from home, a girl staying alone in a new city, but did I have an option?

The apartment door banged on the wall behind me and then I did. Sam was all over me. She had pressed me against the wall so hard that I couldn't even move. Soon I gave up and she took over. Our lips locked, we kissed, so immensely that our hearts were racing faster than that of a panther and we didn't even realize how fast time flew. It was more than 2 hours that I had met her. And we were still in each other's arms, still kissing and loving each other. Though the course of time had shredded off few of our clothes and led us to the bed. We still held on to our limits. It was getting darker outside and I was getting hungry.

"Is there any food in the house? I'm starving." I asked.

"No, we are going out. I have plans for the evening, for the both of us, together!" She replied trying to get off the bed.

"Why can't we just stay here? I like it here, close to you." I replied pulling her back in my arms.

"Don't worry baby. We are going to get back later in the night, on this bed itself ok. Now get up and get ready. We have to leave soon."

Saying this she started getting up, pulling the blanket along with her, hiding the pure divinity of her body. I tried pulling the blanket but it was of no use.

"Later baby, you'll get to see a lot later. Now let go, we need to get ready now." She replied with naughtiness in her voice.

And so I let it go. After an hour of getting dressed up and make up and many questions if she was looking good enough, we left for dinner. Till now the rats in my tummy had starved to death already.

Her car screeched and stopped in front of an Arabian cafe. Her driving was poor but she wasn't going to agree with that. Neither would she have allowed me to drive so instead I quietly sat next to her. We ordered some chicken to eat. I ordered a fruit punch to drink and to this she smirked.

"What happened?" I asked.

She nodded no trying to hide her smile.

"What would you like a drink miss?" The waiter asked her.

"Vodka shot."

"Since when did you start drinking?" I questioned her with concern.

"Since I came here. It's not that bad you know and yes it does give you a high eventually." She replied.

"Sam, come on. You've started changing already." I asked getting more serious.

"Himanshu I've told you that I want to live my life the way I want to. I want to enjoy life and try out everything possible. And so I'm doing it. What's so wrong about that?" Now she had started getting angry.

I couldn't speak after this. It was true. I had liked her for what she was. But I had never seen this side of her, drinking, especially when the shots of vodka kept coming and she didn't stop.

After an hour or so I couldn't take it. I had to stop her. She was losing her brains already. I paid the bill, dragged her towards the car and pushed her in. I was at least happy for the fact that I was driving and wasn't drunk. But the problem was that I didn't know the way to her flat. I had the address stored in my phone. I enquired about the roads and buildings and I got stared by every person I spoke to on the way. Now who wouldn't stare at you if you had a hot chick lying next to you, drunk and unconscious, wouldn't wrong thoughts cross anyone's mind? After a difficult drive of over an hour in the busy roads of Nagpur, we reached back to her apartment. It was on the 3rd floor and obviously she couldn't walk. I carried her all the way up, took her to the bed, and changed her clothes.

After putting her to sleep I walked out of the room into the hall. And spent the rest of the night there, thinking if I was too much into her that I couldn't even see her bad side, couldn't even keep her in control. I was feeling insecure. But there was nothing I could have done and with these thoughts I slowly drowsed away to sleep.

I got up the next morning to find her in my arms. I never realized when she had cuddled up into my arms. At this time I had forgotten about whatever had happened last night. She looked so damn cute while she was asleep; especially in those clothes I had put her into, even though they weren't much. I just lay there, next to her, staring at her, thinking if we still had a chance to talk and work it out.

I looked at my watch and realized it was noon already. I wanted to wake her up, but couldn't. Her spell of cuteness had struck me. I picked her up in my arms careful enough to not wake her up, placed her gently over the bed and then covered her incompletely covered body with a blanket, and kissed her on the forehead.

I took a quick shower, got dressed and was busy in the hall packing my stuff as I had to leave in another few hours. I was unable to find the shirt I had worn last night. I searched over the whole place but couldn't find it. And then I saw it near the bedroom door. The only difference was that it was carrying a beautiful body inside it. It was Sam, wearing my shirt.

"I need the shirt. I have to pack it." I requested Sam.

She walked closer to me and said "Here, unbutton it."

And so I started. Once the top 2 buttons were popped, I realized all she was wearing inside was her skin. My hands were stunned, they couldn't move anymore. And then our lips met again, and then her skin with mine. The shirt flew off and so did the shirt which I was wearing. We were kissing each other and my hands had started to move down from her face to her neck and then to her . . .

Ding dong.

"Fuck!" She exclaimed.

She got up, pulled up some piece of cloth to cover herself as much as she could and ran towards the bed room. And I started searching for both my shirts. It was one of her friends, Divya. I welcomed her in. We spoke for some time, exchanged the general details by the time Sam walked out of the room, only this time completely dressed in jeans and a shirt, her own shirt.

"It's time, I have to go." I said getting up from the couch.

"We'll drop you to the airport." Divya said.

And so we three drove towards the airport. Not many words were exchanged on the way. It was only half an hour left for my plane to fly away when we reached the airport. I had to rush. I put my bag on my back grabbed her hand and pulled her towards myself.

"Listen Sam, I know it's going to be difficult this way but we'll work it out ok." I said.

"Sure we will sweetheart." She replied with a smile.

"But listen. I'm not that comfortable about you drinking so much and staying out late in the night." I said hoping she wouldn't yell at me.

"But Himanshu I thought we decided to let each other live the way we want to. Didn't we?" She asked me.

"Listen Sam, we'll talk about this later. I have to rush now ok!"

And soon my flight took off to Raipur, my home town.

After claiming my luggage, I saw dad as soon as I walked out. He wasn't smiling at all as I had expected him to. He was going to see his son after such a long time but he did not even smile. Did he know what I had just done? But how could he? No way would he know. I walked up to him and touched his feet. He still did not respond. He didn't even say a word. I was feeling weird already.

"Dad what is wrong with you? What happened?" I asked.

"How was a Nagpur?" He asked me without even looking at me.

WHAT? How did he get to know? How could he? Did any of my friends call and tell him? But they couldn't. They didn't even have dad's number. So how was it possible? I knew the half an hour drive to my house was going to be filled with nothing but silence. And so it was.

Even at home mom didn't say a word. Neither did dad. I was feeling worse already. I knew it was their normal parental sentimental drama but I had earned it. I did something to deserve it, and I couldn't complain. I decided to walk up to my room and spend some time there alone. As I was walking to my room across the hall dad said—"We had faith in you."

That was all he said. Not another word. They both had turned and walked away from me. I was alone. They didn't even give me a chance to apologize. For the first time I felt something ache in my chest. For the first time I was really sorry.

What dad had said was more than just a slap across my face and I had not recovered from it yet. But I still wanted to find out how he got to know that I was in Nagpur. During all this time I had even forgotten to switch on my phone after the flight. As soon as I switched it on I got few messages. One of them was from Sam.

"Himanshu, whn v hd startd dis thing bwn us v hd decided tht v wud let each othr live thr life d way v wnt 2, 2do whtevr v wnt 2. Bt nw u r interfering in my life, nw u hv startd havin probs wid my way of living. U r makin me uncomfrtable arnd u. U r nt givin me my space. I cnt wrk dis out dis way. Im sry Himanshu bt dis hs 2 end. Im sorry!"

Why was she doing this? Had she found someone else better? If not, why was she breaking up with me and that too, over a text message? Was she drunk when she sent the message? So many more thoughts crossed my mind but I had something more important to do. I had to call the hostel to find out how dad got to know.

"Hello?"

"Can you call Suraj from 2005 batch?" I requested.

Beep beep beep beep, "Hello?"

"Hey Suraj!"

"Hey Himanshu listen, after you left your dad had called. We told him that you were not around, that you had gone to the bathroom or to play or some other excuse but he kept calling again and again. He said that he had something important to tell. Then he ended up talking to the warden himself and they told your dad that you had left for home already. I'm so sorry man. We tried not to let him know but he spoke to the warden." Suraj narrated the whole story.

"But why did dad call the hostel?" I asked again.

"I have no idea man. I'm so sorry I couldn't help you." Suraj apologized.

"It's ok man. I'll call you back later then ok. Have to speak to dad now." I said ready to keep the phone down.

"Oh so you reached home? How was Sam man? Had fun?" He asked.

"Later Suraj, not now!" I replied.

"Ok fine, take care bro." Suraj said.

"Bye."

So that's how dad had found out. There was no way I could have manipulated the story because dad knew that the warden wouldn't have lied. I was guilty and I couldn't have proved it wrong in any way. I had no other option but to apologize. But they were not going to give me a chance to do that either. I was regretting everything now. A little more because of the message Sam had just sent, and much more because I cared so much and went all the way to Nagpur to meet that bitch.

Later on the same night I got to know why dad wanted to talk to me so badly. Mom and dad were leaving for a conference and they wanted me to come along. Now check this out. The conference was in Nagpur and dad had actually called me to book a flight to Nagpur and meet them there directly. Isn't that so funny? If I had spoken to my dad before leaving I could have spent some more time with Sam and would have never got caught. Life is so messed up, isn't it?

Mom and dad left for Nagpur for the conference and I spent the next 5 days alone at home. Even before they came back it was time for me to leave for the hostel. I wanted to see them at least once before I left, apologize for the stupidity I did. But I didn't have an option. I left home feeling pathetic but determined not to do something this crazy again especially something that would dishonour my dad.

Of all the rarest of things that could happen to someone was to have a beautiful girl sit next to you during a flight which I would usually want to have, but for obvious reasons I didn't even talk to that beauty sitting next to me. I was still depressed and it got even worse when I got back to the college, for one I was away from home once again and secondly I had college the next day. The same pathetic faces of those teachers.

I had joined college the next day itself. I had missed three days earlier already and I didn't want to miss any more. But who knew I would have had to any ways. In the middle of the first class itself the principal's clerk came to call me. I had no clue as to why I was being called. As I reached the office I was handed over a notice. It read like this.

"Himanshu R Patel of 2005 MBBS batch is not allowed to attend classes for breaking the code of conduct and misbehaviour towards the college until further notice."

Signed by the principal.

What was my misbehaviour? That I went to meet my girl without telling my parents? How was it any of their business? But I couldn't argue with them. Not that they would take back the suspension. And moreover the suspension letter was on the notice boards already. Everyone had read it. All the seniors had learned about my suspension.

I was all prepared to get screwed but I was surprised. On my way back up to the class room, which I was going to get my bag, I was congratulated and shook hands by most of the seniors both boys and girls.

"Good job dude, keep it up!"

"Amazing work man, welcome to the group!"

And so on came the compliments.

Were they being sarcastic? But I didn't really care. I went up to my class took my bag and went straight to my hostel room and crashed on my bed, only hoping that mom and dad would call to talk to me, to let me apologize for what I had done.

Chapter Six

"MY SNOW WHITE PRINCESS"

I was suspended for 5 days, which I spent mostly in sleeping and roaming around the city trying to find some good places to hang out. I was disappointed most of the times. Dad called eventually when he got the news that I was suspended. He was angry. I mean angrier. I was shot with mom's sentimental missiles again but somehow I survived those. And the next few days in college went on very well, for I had made many new friends, especially among the seniors. I was known by almost everyone in the college. Getting suspended within the first three weeks of 1st year was a big achievement, something no one ever had the honour of. Nor anyone ever will!

The classes went well. I had started to understand the crap that professors used to blabber. It had all started to make sense. And as the first semester exams were coming closer every day I had started to pay more attention in class. Nothing special was happening in my life for a very long time. The good bye at the airport was the last time I had heard from Sam. Most of my other friends were busy with their courses and the new friends here were not that great that I would share my personal feelings with.

But as they say that everything happens for a reason and so I guess what happened with me was also what god had a reason for. A few weeks before the exams we were asked to go for blood checkups, all the students from the batch. It was for medical records. There I met one of the most beautiful girls I had ever seen in my batch. And she ranked in the top 5 that I had seen so far. Urvashi was her name. She was basically a malayali born and brought up in Delhi, as white as milk, as bright as the sunshine, as charming as a flower and as afraid of a syringe as a cat from water. Yes she was shit scared that day. She was almost screaming outside the procedure room and I knew it better as I was the person right behind her in the line.

She went into the room and after a few seconds of silence I heard a scream. My curiosity made me rush inside the room to see what had happened. The nurse was still holding the needle in her hands and was nowhere close to my new crush. But Urvashi had freaked out already. The nurse asked me for help and I was whole heartedly willing to help with all that I could offer. But the best I could do was to talk to her and at the most hold her hand. That was enough for the first time, right?

"Hey I'm Himanshu!" I started the conversation.

"I know. Who doesn't?" She replied with a smile.

"So how do you like this place?" I continued.

"It sucks to the core." She said making a constipated face.

"I know!" I nodded in agreement.

"So where are you from?" She asked.

"Raipur, and you?" I asked.

"Delhi!" Came the answer.

By the time we exchanged our details the nurse was done with her procedure. Even though the nurse had got enough of Urvashi's blood, I hadn't got enough of her. I needed to know her better. I needed to talk to her more.

"Hey Urvashi, can you do me a favour? Could you stay here for a little while? I'm a little, you know, afraid of needles too." I requested her.

I was lying. I never was afraid. I used to get hurt so often in my childhood and I had so much experience in taking injections that I could give one to myself without any hesitation. The trick worked, she stayed. Though it was very difficult to act scared of something that I wasn't scared of but I somehow managed the whole situation well and even ended up holding her hands, those soft smooth hands.

"Himanshu it's done, let's go." She said pulling my hand.

"Huh? What? Done? But I didn't even feel anything." I tried to act.

"Ha-ha, I know, I didn't either. Come on lets go now." She insisted.

We walked out together, holding hands together. Yeah I wish.

"Hey you want to go to the canteen and get something to drink?" She asked.

"Yeah sure!" Now who could deny that invitation? Her sweet voice, damn!

We sat in the canteen for more than an hour, discussed about so many topics, movies, professors, seniors, college, old friends and many more. And then came the time to part.

"I should get going now. We have to be back before 6 to the hostel." She said.

"Ok carry on. I'll see you in class tomorrow." I replied.

"Hey Himanshu, thanks a lot." She expressed her gratitude.

"For what?" I asked.

"For helping with the blood thing and talking to me. I feel much relieved now." She said taking a deep breath.

"We are friends right? So stick your thanks up yours." I replied tapping her head.

We both smiled and bid goodbye.

The first thing I did when I entered class the next day was to see where she was sitting and then find a seat closest to hers. We started going to the canteen a lot, started exchanging chits in class. I even gave her my phone number so she could call me and then I started getting deprived of my sleep every night. We had started getting close to each other and it felt really good.

Exams were in a few days and nobody knew how soon the days passed by. It was going to start with anatomy, followed by physiology and end with biochemistry. To my bad luck the biochemistry exam was on my birthday. It was my first birthday far away from home. I wasn't thinking much about celebrating it. Most of the people didn't even know about it. On top of that we had exams. So I was sure of saving a lot of money that I would have otherwise spent on treating these nerds especially when dad wasn't sending much.

It was funny how the same corridor where we used to howl and shout and scream everyday turned so silent on the night before the exams. It was as if somebody had died. Everybody was in their rooms all the time; lights never went off in any of the rooms. In the middle of the night you would see people going to the bathroom with a bucket and a book. Everyone was freaking out, it was our first internal exam and we had no idea how to face it. Of course we had some help from the seniors on what and how to study but it was us who were going to face it, right?

I had a senior who I had got along well, Karan. He was one among the gang members who ragged me but he turned out to be one of the most helpful seniors ever. He taught me something called selective study in which you pick out the teacher's most favourite questions and study only those. But how do you find the teacher's favourite questions? That's where the seniors help you. Karan marked all the important questions in my book. His philosophy was that no matter if you pass with 50% marks or 80% you are still going to achieve the same degree and honour. And according to him if you studied all those important questions you would comfortably pass. For our anatomy exams we had embryology and upper limb. Out of the whole set of topics Karan had marked me a total of 36 topics. It took me just two days to finish them, but I was thorough with them. He had given me an equal amount of questions for physiology but he had mentioned that biochemistry is really easy and highly volatile. More over the department and its faculties are lenient with marks, so according to him reading the previous night would be enough. And so I left out biochemistry completely and focused more on physiology as I was weaker in that.

Soon it was the day of anatomy exam. It was from 10 am to 1 pm, 3 hours of torture especially for those who wouldn't know what to write. On the way down Vishnu met one of the seniors.

"Good morning chetan." Vishnu wished the senior.

"All the best da, took everything no?" The senior asked.

"Yes cheta." Vishnu replied with a smile.

"Pencils, scale, colour pencils." The senior asked.

"Colour pencils??" Vishnu asked surprisingly.

"Yes for diagrams!" The senior explained.

"Shit!" He exclaimed.

And he ran back to our corridor and yelled it out loud. Everyone left their books and now was searching for colour pencils. I was into sketching and drawing and so I picked up my set of crayons, cut them into halves so that my roommate could use them also, and we left for the exam together. We were among the first ones to enter the exam hall and the others who entered after us were mostly panting and sweating. At exactly 10 am the question papers were handed over to us.

I finished my paper, submitted and walked out the exam hall at 11.45 am. As nobody else was there to accompany me I came back to the hostel and slept off. A couple of hours later my roommate barged in and started questioning me.

"What were you thinking?" BD asked me.

"Hey how was your paper?" I replied with a question.

"Why did you leave so soon?" He continued asking.

"I was done with the paper." I replied.

"Do you know that all the teachers were looking at your paper and having a discussion? KKK wrote down your name also. I think you'll get in trouble." BD told me.

"For what? I finished my paper so I left. What's the big deal in that? Anyways how was your paper?" I asked.

"Bad!" He said with the expression on his face turning from anger to sadness.

"Why what happened?" I asked.

"I suck at anatomy. Moreover I didn't have time to attempt the last two questions." He replied.

"How come?" I asked.

"I write slow ok. And I wasn't the only one who didn't attempt all the questions. There were many who thought that the paper was very lengthy ok." He responded getting annoyed.

"Ok dude relax." I tried to calm him down.

I hated BD for one reason that he always used to say things that would make me start thinking. Now I was thinking if I wrote enough on the answer sheets. I had seen people take so many extra sheets and writing for the anatomy paper but I didn't take any extra sheets. I just drew lots of colourful diagrams and labelled them. That's all I did. Now I was scared that it wouldn't be enough. I was now sure that I was going to flunk. With this thought in mind I somehow dared to open my physiology book. By this time BD had already changed and was leaving for library.

The next whole day people spent in cramming the whole Guyton, a foreign author textbook. Few of them had followed senior's advice and decided to read AK Jain, an Indian author textbook. And I spent most of my time sleeping. I was nocturnal so I would mostly study at night between 11 and 3. And people thought I didn't study at all. It was funny because they would get more tensed looking at me sleeping most of the time.

Chapter Seven

"Tsunami"

"You have time till 1 pm, that means 3 hours and exactly at 1pm the answer sheets will be taken away." Dr Sebastian said in his cranky voice.

I tried to stay longer this time. It was noon already. I had finished all the answers, as in those which I knew the answers to, drew diagrams and many flow charts. I looked around and caught BD's eyes which gave me an angry stare but I was too bored to sit in that quiet room with so many faces dug into their papers. And so I left.

But this time I wasn't alone. I found many people getting up right after me, and one of them was Urvashi. I crossed my fingers and hoped her paper went well.

We met just outside the exam hall and I found her eyes almost filled with tears. But she didn't cry, we spoke and I tried to console her. Apparently her paper went really bad. I suggested that we started walking away from the hall because Dr Sebastian was giving us angry stares, well maybe they weren't angry stares but his face made it look like they were.

We walked together and spoke for a while.

"My parents would be so disappointed if I fail. I knew the answer to that question, how could I not remember? I think I should go back and start with biochemistry already. I'll call you at night when I take a break ok." She told me.

"Ok!" I agreed.

I walked back to my room and collapsed on the bed.

BD walked in and I said "I stayed in there a little longer today" as if it was some achievement.

He didn't respond.

And so I went back to sleep.

I was woken up by Urvi's call at around 11 pm.

"I'm saturated, nothing more is going in. I can't study any more. So I thought I'd call you, you started?" She asked.

"No." I denied.

And then I told her how seniors think studying just one night before is more than enough for biochemistry. Of course she didn't agree, she thought that I should go study. Of course I changed the topic. We spoke till I realized that all my study time was gone and as soon as we kept the phone I dozed off again.

I woke up around noon the next day, took a bath and went for lunch. When I came back I thought I'll listen to music for some time and then start studying, and while I did that I slept off on my desk. Urvi woke me up around 4 pm.

"Himanshu, can you please talk to me for some time, I'm totally saturated and I can't study a word anymore." She requested.

"Sure, so how much have you finished?" I asked.

"I actually just finished the whole portion once, was planning to start revision soon but I don't think anything will get into my head. How much did you finish?" She asked.

"Actually I was just going to start." I explained.

"What's your plan? What all chapters are you going to do first?" She asked.

"I don't know! Let me open the book first and then I'll decide." I replied.

"Himanshu, do you even know what all chapters are there for the exam?" She asked with the tone of her voice changing.

"Urvi isn't it time for you to go have your tea? I'll give you a call once I take a break ok." I tried to push the topic away.

"Ok fine. But start soon ok." She said.

I hated it when people ask me a lot of questions or when they try to tell me how to do things. Urvi did annoy me at times like this. So I thought I'll go out and get inspired from people studying in the others rooms. Unfortunately most of them were on a break as this was the time when the mess opened up for tea and snacks. Not surprisingly I joined them for their break. After that I spent most of the time goofing around, going to different rooms and asking how much they had finished. While I was crossing Rajesh's room I found him explaining something to his roommate and so I decided to stay in for a moment and listen to what he was blabbering. In amidst of the class I heard my name being announced on the speakers. I had a call!

"Happy Birthday beta! Hope you live for many years and enjoy your life as much as you want!" My Mom wished me.

"Thanks maa." I replied.

"I'm sorry beta, but I don't think I can stay up till 12 to wish you, that's why I thought I'll call you now itself. Your dad isn't back from the hospital yet but he said he'll call you later." She explained.

"It's ok maa, you carry on now. I have to go for dinner and then study for my exam tomorrow." I told her.

"All the best beta!" She wished me.

By the time I got back after dinner and those talks with all the seniors I met on the way, it was almost 10 already. I sat down on my desk but before I opened up my book I thought I'll give Urvi a call.

"Hey, done with your revision?" I asked.

"No, but I'm almost done half way. What about you? How much did you finish?" She asked.

"I'm about to start!" I told her.

"What?? You haven't started yet?? Himanshu what is wrong with you? Keep the phone right now and open up your book. I'm not going to talk to you unless you've finished a good part of the portion for exams tomorrow ok?" She almost yelled at me.

"Ok madam." I replied.

"Now go study! Bye!" She kept the phone.

With a hard struggle, I spent over an hour in front of my books. I somehow managed to finish a chapter when my roommate got back from the library.

"Hey, done with the portion?" I asked BD.

"Almost. What is up with those seniors? They are waiting near the end of our corridor." He questioned.

"I know, even in the mess they were giving me those crazy smiles, maybe it's because of the exams." I presumed and said.

"May be, any ways, I wanted to ask you, did you understand the urea cycle. I tried for so long but I didn't under . . ."

Knock knock.

"Who's it?" BD asked.

"Suraj!"

"Just a sec." I said and I got up to open the door. The second I unlocked the door it was pushed open and a bunch of guys rushed into the room. In split seconds I was lifted off my feet and I was being carried by four people. I was freaking out. I tried to struggle but they were strong. A few seconds later I was dropped right in front of the bathroom as that was the largest area for a group to stand together. As I stood up on my feet I realized I was surrounded by all my seniors and super seniors in a circle. My own batch mates were also there but they formed the outer circle. And then they put a smile on my face. They all sang the birthday song for me, not only my batch mates and seniors but even my super seniors. I felt honoured. But I didn't know this smile was going to turn into screams and pain so soon.

As soon as the song was over I was picked up with all fours again and taken into the bathroom. And then the rapid kicks started, on my bum! Oh god it was painful. Every person over there kicked me at least five times each. Some of them were even wearing shoes. I even remember few of my batch mates jumping in and trying their feet at my ass. I swear after a few seconds my ass went numb and I couldn't even feel a thing. Once all of them were done kicking, my arms and legs were left and I dropped on the floor. Then I heard everybody scream "tsunami tsunami" over and over again. All of a sudden a bucket of steaming hot water was poured over me from behind. I had totally forgotten the torture my ass had gone through by now. And after another round of people chanting "tsunami tsunami" another bucket of water was poured over me. But this time the water was cold, so cold that I literally felt my balls shrink into its sac. And then they all just paused. I was hoping this was all over and I could go change because I was freezing. But it wasn't. Next thing I heard was "Gentlemen . . . aim . . . shoot!!"

And I felt eggs cracking on my head, face, back and god knows where all.

Suddenly one of them came running into the bathroom and the news spread that the warden was on his way up because of all the noise. And within no time I was the only one left there in the bathroom shivering, with broken eggs on my head. I assumed that I was not supposed to say anything to the warden or else I might get into bigger troubles later on. So I was thinking of what excuse I could give him when he questions me. He walked in and before I could say anything he said "oh tsunami again, Ha-ha. Happy birthday, whoever you are!" And he walked away. It had probably become a trend for me to be left speechless every time.

I cleaned up myself and got back to my room, all the while thinking just one question, how did the seniors get to know about my birthday? My bum was hurting so much that I couldn't even sit. No matter how many different positions I tried I couldn't sleep. So I decided to study.

"The exam is of 2 hours only unlike other 2 subjects so please finish it in time."

The question paper was easy, may be for the fact that I had studied last night. I did my regular stuff, flow charts, diagrams, and I was done with my paper in an hour. At 11.15 I got up to leave the exam hall. A lot of people following my lead didn't surprise me this time. Because the reason I left so early wasn't the same as theirs. This time I knew the answers to most of the questions, and that too the correct answers. It was just that I had to finish my paper as soon as possible because I couldn't take myself sitting on my ass; it was hurting really bad from last night.

"Hey how was it?" I asked Urvashi.

"It was ok. How was . . . Himanshu did you eat egg? Wait . . . you are stinking of egg . . . Himanshu what did you do??"

And then I explained the whole tsunami that happened last night.

"Oh my God, why didn't you tell me? Happy birthday Himanshu!" Wishing that to me, she hugged me!

It felt good. Everybody else was staring at me but for some reasons it didn't make a difference to me. I wasn't embarrassed. It wasn't awkward at all. And most surprisingly my ass wasn't hurting even a little bit.

"So how come you told your seniors but not me?" She asked pulling my cheeks.

"That's the thing I don't understand. I never told anybody. I have no idea how they found out!" I explained my confusion.

"Forget it. So how are you planning to celebrate your day?" She asked me.

"I have no plans so far." I said.

"I wish we could go out somewhere but we are not allowed to." She said in a low tone.

"I know. It's ok. How about we just go get lunch for starters?" I suggested.

"Ok." She agreed.

We sat in the canteen together, had our lunch. Then we went to juice stall, spoke to each other till around 4 pm when my second round of embarrassment started. The seniors had done enough damage last night but it wasn't enough from the seniors. The girls hadn't had their chances yet. Though their way wasn't tough on my ass but it sure was on my wallet. Yes they sang a birthday song for me, and many of them pulled my cheeks and gave me hugs and wished me, but the amount they ate, oh my god! If we had to donate that much amount of food we might have saved half the percentage of people dying from starvation, all over the world.

After being mugged by my senior girls when I got back to the hostel I found that it was back to the way it used to be a few weeks ago. Everybody was in everybody else's room. There was so much noise that you couldn't hear someone standing next to you. But all this felt great. I got back to my room and called home to tell mom about the natural disaster that happened to me.

"Hello, mom?" I asked.

"What is wrong with your warden? Every time we call and ask for you, that idiot connects to some Himanshu from 2004 batch." Dad replied!

"Last night also the same thing had happened before I wished him. I ended up wishing someone else." Mom screamed in the background.

This is when it clicked me on how my seniors would have found out. We spoke for a quite long time considering describing them the tsunami wasn't that easy. And then to convince my mom not to complain about it was also a difficult task. Worse than that was to tolerate her mom stuff. Are you ok? Did you catch cold? Did you use shampoo?

Suddenly I heard everybody crowding up in the corridor and I had to bid mom and dad goodbye. We had all gathered in the corridor when some super seniors came to make some announcements. They were here to invite us to the arts festival they were hosting next weekend. They told us about all the different events that were going to be there. Now there was a new thing that was going to distract us for quite some time. Fortunately many people, who were depressed from the fact that their exams had gone really bad, now had reasons to cheer up as the results would definitely not be out in the next two weeks. That meant that we could all enjoy freely and our parents couldn't complain about it. But there was something that bothered all of us. I mean we all had seen how bad this college was, with all the restriction and rules. It was just that none of us knew what to expect from the first arts festival that we were going to take part in!

Chapter Eight

"Is this thing on?"

Instead of an inauguration dance or a song the arts festival started with the principal giving us a speech on how to not overwhelm ourselves and cause troubles to ourselves and others. Then Arunaji, the head of our mess gave a long speech in Sanskrit which none of us understood. Then followed the event of cultural solo dance competition in which many girls dressed in typical traditional clothes with loads of jewelleries and makeup to dance on some classical music. It was definitely good dancing but none of us were up for classical stuff. The next event for the day was classical singing and instruments. We were all prepared for a long boring session with ridiculous songs to be sung by different people but one of our seniors came up on stage and totally surprised us. We all diverted our attention to the stage for the first time in the entire day as we had all heard that he was the funniest guy from our senior batch.

"Hey guys this is Ajith Kambhi. And as the situation over here is getting uncontrollably boring I was told to lighten the situation. I'm going to tell you guys a joke or rather a short story and that's about it. So here it goes. Once upon a time there was this boy who enjoyed his life in this college." And then he just paused.

The whole crowd was just silent. Most of us didn't respond because of the fact that the principal was sitting on the first row and he didn't have an expression on his face after that joke. For some reason he immediately got up and left the hall. The second the door closed behind him the crowd burst out into laughter. The boring session of classical singing continued and after a while another senior, this time a girl came up on stage to entertain us.

"Hey guys, no I'm not going to tell you any funny stories but I assure you that this is going to be fun. Well for a very small part I need four guys up here on stage, one from each batch. Now hurry up and send me those four guys up here."

The music started in the back ground and we all thought it would be something to do with dance. So from my batch I was pushed forward. I got on to the stage with 3 seniors and the girl started speaking again.

"Well we all would like to see some nice ramp walk on the stage won't we?" The girl asked the crowd.

And the crowd screamed yes in chorus.

For some reason I started feeling something fishy about the whole thing. Just making us walk on the stage like that wouldn't be so funny.

The girl turned to us and said "guys you have one minute to prepare and then you are going to walk on the ramp."

"Prepare for what?" The senior next to me asked.

That second four girls walked to us from the side of the stage each carrying a saree for the four of us. We were supposed to wear a saree in less than a minute and then walk on the ramp. All four of us were shocked and surprised.

"Time is running out guys!" The girl with the mic acknowledged us.

My senior immediately picked up the saree and started wrapping himself into it. We all knew we had to do it anyways so the rest three of us started with the sarees as well. A minute was over and it was time for the cat walk. The senior most guy turned to the ramp and started walking. After his first two steps his saree went lose and he tripped on the stage and fell on his back. The crowd roared with laughter and he ran off the stage pulling up his saree with a blushing face. The next guy picked up his saree and walked the ramp. It was very awkward as all he focussed on was not falling and somehow completed his walk soon. He did not get much of a cheer from the crowd even though it looked very ridiculous and funny. Next was my turn. I had wrapped around the saree, made pleats out of it and tucked it into my belt, so there was no chance of me tripping over it. I slowly walked in a straight line crossing my next step before the first one and reached the edge of the ramp. To win the competition I had to do something but I wasn't sure of what to do. I turned around and started walking back. I stopped half way turned around and gave a naughty look and a flying kiss to the crowd and then walked back. I did get a lot of cheers from the crowd but it was nothing compared to what my senior did next. Even before I reached back he started his walk. He made a fast walk all the way to the front and stood balancing his wait mostly on his back foot with his hand resting on his hip. He looked like a professional model that walked on the ramp every day. As soon as his stance was over and he was about to turn around, his palloo fell off his shoulders. He said "oops" really loud and then picked up his palloo and pushed it back on the shoulders. Keeping his hand on the middle of his chest, he smiled and blushed like a girl as if his cleavage was exposed. He then walked back a little and then turned his head around, kept his hand on his bum and gave a very, very dirty look to the crowd and then walked all the way back to stand by my side. The entire crowd was cheering the whole time and we all knew who the winner was. The girl declared him as the winner and he was given a round of applause from the crowd and we got off the stage. That was the only fun thing that happened on the first day of the arts festival. Our batch had so many expectations from our seniors, but we were not touched by the first day. We were only hoping for things to improve the next day.

The next day's first event was shipwreck. In this game you are given a personality's name which you have to in act and give reasons as to why you should be the first person to be saved from a wrecking ship. Many of our seniors acted first for different characters of the movies, politics, sports and many more. This game needed a lot of spontaneity and courage to act on stage. So from our batch there was only one guy who participated. Sanil, as his name was, was a short, actually very short, dark guy from US and was known to be very funny but we hadn't seen any of his humorous activities on the stage yet. He went up on stage and picked a chit which read "Britney spears". He was given a minute to prepare and we all were sure he was not going to be able to do much as it was a female character. A minute later he walked up on stage and the judges asked him why she should be the person to be saved first.

"Because I'm Britney, don't you know me? I'm the icon of pop and there are no better females around here anyways. I'm hot and sexy and we can work things out, if you know what I mean, he said winking at the judges."

We were all surprised how he could have made such a statement on the stage. Fortunately none of the administrative people were around and that meant that the fun wasn't going to stop. The question answer session went on for a little while when the judges confessed that they needed a better reason to save her first.

He then took the mic in his hands and turned away from the crowd. For a few moments he was busy with something which we thought was preparation to give a good answer. But when he turned around we were all shocked.

He took the mic closer to his mouth and started singing.

"Hey, is this thing on?"

He turned around with that line and what we saw looked like a man slut. His shirt buttons were all open and the lower end was tied into a knot which rested right below his boobs, well if he had boobs the knot would have been right under them. His manly hairy chest and his flabby abdomen were exposed. He had messed up his hair and looked like a funny joker from a circus. He continued with the song "I love rock and roll" one of the most famous songs by Britney Spears. While singing he did many vulgar steps which also included bending forwards and holding his chest and trying to expose his imaginary boobs to the judges. But the last one step was probably the one which got him the second prize in that competition. He pulled a chair from the crowd and sung louder sitting on it. He then got off the chair and while singing slapped his own ass with a very naughty look on his face, the same way Britney did in her song video. The crowd went crazy on this move and the judges nodded with a smile and told him that it was enough. He untied the knot and buttoning his shirt got off the stage. The crowd welcomed him with a lot of cheers; especially our batch girls and we continued waiting for the end of the program for announcement of the results. Sanil had performed very well and for the same he scored a 2ⁿᵈ prize.

We were all happy for he was the first one from our batch to win something. But we were not going to be satisfied with just one prize. The boy's group dance competition was to be conducted as the last event of the next day and we had been up the whole night practicing for the same. I had been dancing since my school days and was the only person who had performed on a stage before. So for reasons very obvious I was picked to take charge of the group dance. As we did not know the whole batch very well yet, it was very difficult for me to pick a group. But I had to manage with whoever I had and prepare. We went up on stage with least preparation in a group of five people out of which four of them had never danced before in their entire life. So it was difficult for us to even stand a chance for a prize but like always I got lucky. There were a total of three groups performing and only one prize was to be given. The senior most group was the best one but had a terrible wardrobe malfunction which knocked them out of our way. The second potential competitors were our senior batch. But during their dance, two of their performers clashed and fell on the stage. That left us and only us for the competition. All we had to do was to perform without any gross mistakes and we would have the title. Moreover towards the end of our group dance I made a small solo performance which grabbed the crowd's attention as well as that of the judges. The results were announced and we were jumping up and down with joy for it was our first victory in this college. Many people congratulated me but the one that I felt precious was the hand shake I got from Urvashi.

"That was awesome Himanshu!" Urvashi exclaimed.

"Thanks." I replied catching my breath.

"So are you happy?" She asked.

"Of course I am!" I replied.

"You want to go get some water? You look thirsty." She suggested.

"Yup, that will be great." I replied.

"Let's go, I'll come with you." She said with a smile.

We got out of the auditorium and headed for the drinking water area. On the way and even while I was drinking water she kept appreciating me for the way I had danced. But on the way back she had a disturbing question to ask me.

"Hey Himanshu, do you know that guy who performed Britney Spears on stage yesterday, Sanil?" She asked.

"Yeah, why?" I questioned her in return.

"No I was just asking. How is he as a person?" She asked further.

"Yeah he is nice, but why are you asking like that?" With a worrying look on my face I asked her.

"Just like that. One of my friends wanted to know that's why." She answered.

"Oh ok. Though he has some attitude and ego issues but otherwise he is a nice guy. He is funny too." I responded.

"Yeah I know. Anyways the ending ceremony of the arts fest is about to start. I'm going to go sit with the girls now. I'll give you a call sometime later ok." And she walked away.

The arts fest was like a short wonderful dream. Even before we had realized it started it had to end. Every single person in the whole class was still hung over with the loads of fun we had during arts and none of the faces carried a smile. The smile less faces were so, for two reasons, one the arts fest was over and secondly because our exams results were to be declared today. The Morning Prayer was over and Dr Sebastian with his gang of professors was ready to distribute our papers of physiology. Of all the days we had seen him, we never knew that his ugly face could wear a smile but this was the day when he had a smile on his face. One by one roll numbers were called and papers were handed over by Dr Sebastian along with comments that started flow of tears from a lot of eyes, especially girls. "You should consider going back home and give more attention to cooking and household work because you are no good here", "You really think you have what it takes to be a doctor?", "You are just not meant to be here", "You worked really hard to show that you don't know anything" were few of his comments. And for people who scored really high percentage, he would tell them that it wasn't enough, or that it is less than half of what they can do. Just because these professors have the brains and managed to pass MBBS, they act like big shots and screw the rest of the generations.

"This exam was nothing but a big joke to you all, wasn't it? But let me tell you one thing you foolish bunch of irresponsible immature kids, if this is what is going to happen in the next coming exams, I promise you that your duration in this college will indefinitely prolong and all that will ever be a joke is your life and nothing else." and he walked out.

Even before we could accept our failures, professors from biochemistry department walked in with the papers. The roll numbers were called again but this time no comments or taunts were attached. Papers were given off silently. At the end the HOD stood up and said "This was your first exam of the many you are going to face in the next five years. We understand that you are not ready for all this yet. But its time you forget your childhood past and start taking up responsibility of yourselves and start studying. The next exams are going to be harder and it will be more difficult to score marks. Some of you have passed with really good marks, congrats to them. Some of you barely made through the border, you need to work harder. And those of you, who didn't make it through this time, don't get depressed. Just make sure that you keep giving in your best efforts and trust me, you will evolve as the best doctors this institute will ever produce. All the best to everybody." and she too with her staff, left.

We were told by our seniors that biochemistry dept has the friendliest staff that we will ever come across. The HOD just proved the point. Many wet faces had dried up, though few of them continued crying. Pushing these thoughts aside I got up to look for that one soul who could console me. Not that I needed to be consoled. Even though I had scored just above the pass percentage, I was one amongst those very few bastards who had passed both the subjects, and anatomy was my strongest subjects in which I was sure to pass. I was happy for myself but concerned about what her scores were. I remember how her face was at the end of each exam. And there she was occupying one of the corner seats at the end of the row. She wasn't crying but her face was all red. I sat next to her and before I could say anything she said "Don't say anything, just sit here ok."

I nodded in agreement and sat right next to her. In the next few minutes the anatomy team barged into the lecture hall with papers. Urvi looked up with disappointment and went back to staring at her feet. We thought that nobody could beat Dr Sebastian in sadism and cruelty. But our cheerful smiling colourful HOD had a lot more for us then just giving away our marks. There were four staff members from the dissection hall who sprinted between the tables distributing respective papers to everybody. As soon as the distribution was over the front lights were switched off and the projector was started. The presentation was titled "The funniest moments of my life by Dr KKK". Pictures of our theory papers popped up one by one. Not every ones papers were there in the presentation, only the ones who had made blunders and big mistakes. One by one she flipped through the slide show commenting on them and laughing out loud. With every comment she made the whole anatomy department staff joined her in her laughter. The rivers that Dr KKK started this time were unstoppable and people inconsolable. The last slide of the presentation read.

"The End, Thank you for these laughs, hope you will make us laugh again in the next semester exams"

And the laughing monsters left the hall leaving behind wet faces gasping for breath. Those who were a little stable were consoling the weaker ones, even though it was very obvious that everyone needed a tissue.

After a long stare at her feet, her eyes shed a single drop of crystal clear tear which rolled down her white now turned red cheeks. I wiped the tear off her face, pulled her head into my chest and hugged her, and she lost control over her eyes.

It was the same scene all over the lecture hall. Many people were hugging each other and crying. Most of them were saying something to console those crying faces but in my stupid head nothing was coming up that I could say to make her feel better. She had failed all three subjects and was crying her eyes out in my arms and I could not think of anything to comfort her. The only thought that crossed my mind was if the eyeliner that she was wearing would stain my white shirt or not.

The next many days of our lectures were silent. The only idiot talking was on the Dias making complicated gestures which no one cared to focus on. But that was not what I was concerned with. It had been days since I had called Urvi. She had told me in class not to come up and speak to her because that would make her breakdown again. "I'll call you when I feel better, ok." were the last words I'd heard from her in days. Finally after a week I couldn't take it anymore and gave her a call.

"Hello?"

"Hey, I was just about to call you Himanshu. Listen I need your help. We girls have decided to do group study from now on so that we all can improve. But they are doing only biochemistry and physiology. Anatomy is your stronger subject, can you help me please?" She requested.

"Of course I will. Why are you even asking? Just let me know when you want to start ok." I replied.

"I was thinking I can study with the girls in the hostel even at night. So you can teach me anatomy right after class in the library till 6. Is that ok?" She asked.

"Sure, when do you want to start?" I asked.

"Is tomorrow ok with you? I really want to prepare well for the next exams." She asked.

"Ok, so I'll meet you after class tomorrow." I responded.

"Himanshu, I love you" and after a short pause she said "for helping me out like this."

"Only for helping you?" I asked trying to tease her.

"I'll see you tomorrow Himanshu" she said with a giggle "And you can start bothering me again in class now, I miss all that."

And setting my love train back on the right track, I bid her goodnight.

Chapter Nine

"MY CHRISTMAS WHAT?"

It had been over 2 weeks since results were out. Many had stabilized. Many had started studying like there is nothing more to life. But on the other hand for me and Urvi getting angry and 'I know what you both are up to' stares from seniors, professors and staff members especially security guards was a very regular thing now. But that didn't bother either of us anymore. We used to sit on the steps right in front of the library immediately after classes till 6 pm, every single day. My face had a reason to smile every day now. No matter how many times I used to get yelled at or thrown out of class, at the end of the day I would have spent about two hours with her, every single day. Moreover I had to study myself so that I could teach her, that way my academics, along with my love life, kept moving forward.

"Hey u free tmrw? V cn study al day 2gethr?" A message blinked on my phone from Urvashi.

"Bt tmrw is Sunday!☹ n library wud b closed" I replied.

"Cumon Himanshu, v cn study on d stairs in frnt of d library. V cn spend mre time 2gethr"

And her next message read "mre time studying"

I smiled and replied "Ok fine. Whn do u wana strt?"

"V'l strt by 8 in d mornin. Tht way by evenin v cn evn strt a lil bit of wht is gona b tot on Mon." her text read.

"Bt 8 in d morning is too early. I wudnt evn wake up!" I replied with a lot of concern.

"I'l cal at 7.30 2 wake u up. Goodnight." She replied.

"Fine gudnyt" was my last text to Urvashi before I slept off.

I had never woken up this early on any of the Sundays since I passed out of my school. But I didn't regret it as it was for a good cause, plus waking up to her voice would be blissful.

We sat next to each other the whole day, had breakfast and lunch together, covered up most of the portions taken in class so far. We even went through the topic that was to be taken the next day. While we did all this, time flew by us without even arousing any suspicion. It was past 4 pm already and she got up to drink some water from her water bottle kept 4 steps below. The whole time we sat next to each other without leaving any gap even for air to pass. We kept books on each other's lap and used both of them to study. There were times when her hands would touch my hands or tummy and there were even more times when my hands would go off the books, of course accidentally. Obviously it was very difficult for me to concentrate the whole time and that is why this brake was so much more of a relief for me.

Once she was done quenching her thirst, she walked up the steps just in front of me. Attaining a distance which was just within my reach, she bent forwards to confound my eyes deep below her neck and placed her palm on my cheek. Her pink lips which were still wet from the water she drank slowly moved towards mine. Sweat started appearing on my forehead and her beautiful eyes glanced straight into mine. We were about to kiss.

"Himanshu what are you looking at?" she exclaimed while she was bent forwards running her hands through my hair trying to wake me up from my day dream.

"Why are you sweating?" She asked.

"No, nothing. Come on now, let us get started again." I replied.

"Don't you think we've had enough for the day?" She asked me while she placed herself right behind me one step higher, but still close to me.

"But I thought you wanted to study all day today?" I asked.

Placing her hands around my neck and shoulders sliding them forwards she said "Can I ask you something?"

"Sure, go ahead." I replied with a shiver in my voice.

"What were you staring at?" By now one of her hands was playing with the top most buttons of my shirt and her other hand was on my neck slowly decreasing my comfort level.

"What, no I wasn't staring at . . ." while I was trying to clarify myself and lie to her, she pushed my chin up pulling my face closer to hers, her other hand slid inside my shirt bypassing the limits, her soft silky hair fell forwards covering my face. She gently placed a kiss on my forehead giving me a level of comfort which I could have never attained myself. It was like a déjà vu. I had dreamt of what was going to happen now a million times over and over again. Her lips were moving forward, to place a kiss where I wanted it! Everything around was so silent. The only thing I could hear was her breath, and my heart that was pounding like a horse. To break the silence, from nowhere I heard a giggle, it wasn't me and neither was it her.

Suddenly two seniors, a guy and a girl ran up the stairs, clearly they were not here to study. The girl was wearing a salwar suit but her dupatta was wrapped around the guys hands, his shirt's top buttons were open and the girl's hair was a mess. On top of all this, both were sweating, tremendously. On realizing they weren't alone the guy tried to pull up his shirt straight and the girl tried to un-mess her messed up hair. Their giggle stopped but they continued to go up the steps. They crossed us and gave both of us a wicked smile. And a few seconds later there were more giggles and sounds listening to which we decided that it was time for us to leave.

While picking up all our books our hands touched each other a lot, and just like those stupid Bollywood movies we gave each other those naughty but cute glances. We packed up our bags and started climbing down the stairs. On the walk down she held my hand, really tight. On the first floor, just before we were going to enter an area where we wouldn't be completely alone any more, she turned towards me, got on her toes and placed a kiss on my cheek.

"I'll see you in class tomorrow, ok. And yeah, thanks." And she walked away to her hostel leaving me behind, lost, in her eyes, in those kisses, in her thoughts.

That night we spoke over the phone, but neither of us brought up or questioned about what had happened today. It was a very normal conversation which did not even last that long. Soon she wished me goodnight and went to sleep. But with her thoughts in my head, it took me a very long time to fall asleep.

The next morning still hugging my pillow tight I woke up to an empty room with the door wide open. Somehow I carried myself to the door and noticed all the other doors locked from outside. It took me just another second to understand that I had over slept realizing which I looked at my watch. 9:45 it read which meant I had just enough time to attend dissection. I hurried and rushed my way to the dissection hall and reached just 2 steps ahead of my table teacher. She was an assistant professor, Dr Sindhu and she was Suraj's aunt, the reason why he was so relaxed and wore a big smile on his face. She parked her giant rear on a stool and all of us idiots assembled around the table trying to take a peek on what she was going to teach. She picked up the scalpel and stabbed the dead body on its left thigh, just missing, by few inches, the most important anatomical structure of a male human body which in general terms we call "the Balls". Dragging the scalpel down towards the knee, with utmost brutality, she sliced through the entire thickness of the skin as if it was a fruit. After making more brutal cuts, some near the sac of man-ness and some near the knee, she held a white colour strap like structure, pulled by her forceps and said.

"This is th . . . ."

And with her mighty arms she pulled out the white strap like thing out of the dead body, probably by mistake and continued ". . . the femoral nerve."

She pointed out a few more structures in the femoral triangle, which did not seem to have any geometrical correlation to the shape of a triangle. After many pokes and many more Greek words that vomited out of her mouth, pointing aimlessly she commanded—"You and you, dissect the other leg. I will return after 30 minutes and we all shall revise what we have learned so far."

After her giant rear overloaded a chair in the distant corner of the hall, we all started looking at each other's faces trying to find out the 2 idiots who would step up and do the dissection. For the fact that I had read about it yesterday with Urvashi I stepped up along with Sanil. I quickly remembered him as the guy who Urvashi asked me about during the arts fest but then again I tried to focus on the dissection as rarely it happens that I know something that's going on in the class. After 30 minutes of sweating foreheads, patience and precision we finished dissection of the femoral triangle of the right side. The structures were clearly visible and for a difference the femoral nerve was still intact. After the dissection we both sat down and were reading our books making sure that we hadn't missed any structure, when we heard her steps approaching our table. Suddenly Suraj, who was busy till now acting cool and smart as the teachers relative, got up to pick up a pair of forceps and started describing the structures to the girls sitting next to him.

"What are you doing? What is this? Oh my god, you call this dissection? All you have done is butchered into this human's body who donated his life so that you could learn. And you have wasted such a good specimen."

Unfortunately Suraj was pointing structures on the left side on which madam had done the dissection herself. It was done in such a hurry that it did look like it was butchered.

For a second she took a pause and we thought she was going to teach us something for real now. But her machine gun mouth started again.

"Suraj you think this arrogance of yours is going to get you anywhere? You are mistaken. With the amount of superiority complex you have, you are going to reach nowhere. Look at this; I have dissected the right side so beautifully and neatly. Every structure is visible and recognizable easily. The femoral artery, the femoral vein and the . . ."

She was about to say the femoral nerve. But then it struck her that she had chopped off the femoral nerve while she was doing the dissection herself. She was as if her voice ran away from her. She took a pause, dropped the pair of forceps she was holding and walked away saying "It's time for attendance. We will do this topic tomorrow again more properly. All of you should read and come."

All of us at the table who were trying to hide their giggles burst out into laughter as soon as she was out of the vicinity. I and Sanil were appreciated for our dissection and we settled down on our stools silently for the attendance with a smile on our faces. This was the first time I had a proper conversation with Sanil, the guy who was famous for his humour, the guy who my Urvashi enquired about.

"So who is your Christmas friend?" Sanil enquired.

"My Christmas what?" I was puzzled.

"Didn't you come in the morning? Just before we came down to the dissection hall we picked up our Christmas friends. Don't you know the game?" He asked.

Then he explained me how we pick lots to find our Christmas friend and then you can ask them to do any dare as you wish and that person has to do it.

"Similarly you will be somebody's Christmas friend and you will get dares to do. But remember, at the end of the whole game you will have to buy your Christmas friend a gift. Now go to the class rep and pick up a lot and find out who your Christmas friend is." He explained further.

"Ok thanks." I replied.

On our way to the mess hall for lunch, I met the class rep and picked up my Christmas friend. It was a girl named Swapna, a name I vaguely remembered writing on the list I made for my seniors but I could not recollect her face which made it pretty obvious to me that she wasn't that great looking.

It was the last day at college before the Christmas holidays and everyone was ready and excited to leave for home. Also this was the day when all the dares of the Christmas friend were to be performed. The whole class was filled with the same crowd as always but there was something different. BD had a different hairstyle, Ramu had his moustache shaved off, and Suman had no hair on his head. These were those few dares which had to be done before coming to class. But there were many more to be performed during class. Swapna, who was my Christmas friend had to tie two pony tails like a school girl with ribbons, wear her right shoe on her left foot and her left shoe on the right foot and change seats during the class at least three times. We heard her sandals make a lot of noise while she ran to change her seats. The professor turned around every time to see what the noise was but as he turned towards the crowd there would be pin drop silence. And the second he looked away there would be the loud footsteps of Swapna. While she was doing her task I received a chit which was the dare I was supposed to do. I was to hold my ears and stand up on my chair and do sit ups five times before the teacher left the class. After a while when the teacher started to rub off the fully filled black board with a duster, I quickly stood up on the chair and started doing sit ups with my ears held in my hands. I quickly successfully finished my task and was about to take my seat when the professor turned around and caught me just before I was about to sit.

"Yes, what is your doubt?" The teacher asked.

I was surprised. I didn't expect to get caught.

"No doubt sir." With a lot of hesitation I said.

"So why are you standing?" He questioned me again.

"I was going to sit down sir." I replied.

"But why did you stand up in the first place?" Now he was getting annoyed.

"Hmm I was just adjusting my pants sir." Pulling up my pants I said.

"Maybe next time you want to adjust something you should get out my class. Now shut up and sit down." He replied angrily.

This way the class went on. We saw a paper plane flying from the left side of the classroom to the right side fortunately missing the professor's eyes. Papers rolled into balls were flying from left to right and vice versa. There were many more dares going on but it was too difficult to keep a track of all of them. Finally the professor finished his class and left after attendance. Suraj swiftly ran to the computer and played an Arabic song on the speakers and Sunil ran up to the stage with the mic in his hands.

"Hey guys, this is Sunil and I'm going to perform my task which will probably be the last one as its four already. So I'll be quick. I don't know who this ridiculous person is who has asked me to do a belly dance on stage but as I've learned that I cannot back out from this, I'm going to entertain you guys as much as I can."

The music started on the speakers and Sunil started shaking his hips and his belly started bouncing. I got up and tied my apron around my waist and jumped on to the stage too. Soon many more guys and girls ran up to the stage and we danced our hearts out in the lecture halls for the first time to an Arabic song.

Sunil's dance was the last task for this year's Christmas friend celebration, especially after all of us had joined him to make it a big belly dance show.

It was already past 4, and most of us were getting late for our flight or whatever means of transport we had booked our tickets for. In that big crowd rushing out of the lecture hall, I lost my snow white princess somewhere. But as I was in a hurry like everyone else, I too, had to rush. On my way running to the hostel two very important things crossed my mind. For one I was going face my dad after almost 6 months of not talking properly over the phone, and secondly I did not have Urvi's Delhi number. How the hell was I going to contact her for the next two weeks?

After a pathetic flight of one and a half hours I landed in Raipur. While I was collecting my baggage I was supposed to be happy but instead my mind was going through a lot of mixed thoughts. What if dad was here to pick me up? What if I don't get to talk to Urvi for the next 2 weeks? How will I greet him? What if she finds another guy in Delhi? What if he is still angry on me with whatever had happened with Samyukta? I wish Urvi was here right now! Focus Himanshu!! Stop thinking so much.

Somehow I managed to give my mind a slap of peace and walked out to find my mom waiting for me. As always her eyes almost filled up with tears. I bent down to touch her feet and she gave me a tight hug. She was carrying a giant purse and I knew it had something for me. As soon as we got into the car she opened up that giant sac and took out a couple of boxes filled with puri and paneer, some of my favourites.

"Mom, drive to our house is only 30 minutes from here, I could have had it at home na?" I asked her.

"Nahi beta, I thought you'd be hungry, you travelled so much na?" Her love spoke.

"It was only an hour and a half long flight!" I replied.

"Now stop arguing and eat." She ordered.

As I tore the first bite n dipped it into some edible curry, considering what I had in the hostel mess was equivalent to crap, something started bothering me. I dropped the food back into the box and turned towards mom.

"He is still angry with me isn't he?" I asked.

"Himanshu, forget all that, I'm sure you are hungry. Don't you want to eat?" She tried to change the topic.

"Don't divert the topic maa, tell me!" I insisted.

"Himanshu, promise me one thing, when we reach home you are not going to mention any thing that had happened in the last 6 months, not about your Nagpur trip, not about your suspension. Not even to me. Ok?"

"Fine, now tell me, have you brought any pickle or not?" And this way I decided to keep my mouth shut.

We reached home before I could finish eating. Any how we entered the house but dad wasn't there. Mom inquired and later told me that he was still stuck up in the hospital with some case. And so I had another filling dinner number two and headed to my dream world which was the only place at present where I could at least appreciate the beauty of my princess. My sleep wasn't pleasant. I kept waking up in the middle of the night several times, sometimes by the sweet dreams of my Urvi, and sometimes by the nightmares of my dad.

To face my dad and speak to him properly I woke up in time and was ready by 9 am for breakfast as that was the time dad usually comes down for breakfast. But to my surprise and disappointment he had already left.

At this point I had lost all hopes of getting back the perfect father son relation I had once upon a time with my dad. The yummy French toast my mom had made for me almost seemed tasteless. To top it all I still had no means to contact Urvi. As expected I spent the whole week sleeping, eating, sleeping, watching movies, eating, sleeping, eating, sleeping and of course missing Urvi. After a week of no see no talk treatment from my dad he finally decided to speak to me. This afternoon he came home and knocked on my door while I was watching 'Terminator 2' in full volume. I hustled, tripped on the wires, struggled a lot to switch off the sound and reached the door, opened it and found dad ready to knock again. Suddenly, the hard rough slap which he had given me 6 months ago imprinted on my mind once again.

"If you are not too busy I would like to talk to you in the hall." He said.

What was he going to talk about? Did I do something wrong again? Did he find out about Urvashi? Is he going to slap me again? With all these head banging thoughts I changed into more descent clothes and walked into the hall where he was sitting on the couch waiting for me. I guess I was supposed to sit on the couch he was staring at.

I slowly walked to the couch and placed myself on it, sitting like a little girl who had just made a big mistake, legs clamped together with hands between them, head down and eyes shut.

With a brief period of silent awkwardness he initiated the conversation.

"So how is it there, in your college? Having any troubles?" He asked.

"No, it's going fine." I replied with a husky voice.

"Your mother told me that you passed your sessional exams, all three subjects. Did you really?" He questioned.

"Yes I did!" I replied widening my chest.

"That's good, so you are getting back on track. That's really good. I hope you are not going to trouble me with another girl issue of yours in that college." His voice seemed to have some sort of relief now.

"No dad why will . . . Tring tring tring "Hello?" Dad answered the call.

"Yes he is here. May I know who this is speaking?" He spoke.

"Just a minute. You will never change will you?" Handing the phone over to me with anger he walked out of the hall. I didn't understand a thing. I mean he was right here the previous second trying to make a proper conversation with me. Then what happened suddenly?

I picked up the phone and "Mmmmwwwaaahhhhh!!! How are you Himanshu, do you know how difficult it was for me to find your number? And why is your Kochi number switched off?"

"Urvashi? How did you . . . why did you . . . I mean . . . you know what . . . I'm in the middle of something right now, I'll call you back ok."

And I slammed the phone down and rested my head on my palms starring at my feet.

Why is my life so messed up? Why do right things go wrong at the right times? Oh my god this stupid landline doesn't have a caller identity, how am I going to call back Urvashi. Damn it dad is coming back, another slap for sure this time.

But for my safety he walked across me straight out of the house. And then again my irregularly regular cycles of sleeping, eating and movies continued till I reached the airport for my departure from Raipur.

Chapter Ten

"WILL YOU BE MY VALENTINE?"

Everything wasn't back to normal in the lecture halls yet. Every time a student stood up to ask a question to the teacher, the crowd would stare at him as if he got up to do a task from his Christmas friend. I had realized one thing here, all the good things come to an end very soon, so live it and love it as much as you can. And also every good thing was followed by a very bad one. For example the fog of our happy holidays still surrounded all of us which were soon defogged by the notice which had dates for our second sessional exams. But this time for a change I and Urvi were prepared. All the hard work, especially from my side, now had a chance to pay off. But the brutality of these exams was that it started on the 15th of Feb. I was anxiously waiting for the 14th Feb as I had decided to go official with Urvashi, finally. Now the days seemed longer, professors did not stop barking in any of the classes, our breaks were shortened, dissection hours were stricter, and the hours I spent after class with Urvashi also reduced as both of us used to get too tired after the whole day. Because of this new stupid schedule I had less time to complete all the things I was planning to make for my other half on this Valentine's Day. But somehow I managed to make a lot of things to surprise her. By the end of 12th Feb I had a big white chart which read 101 reasons why I loved her, 14 flowers made out of paper, a couple of paintings and sketches which depicted nothing but love. I had already bought her a pendent and a bracelet and a lot of chocolates were due to be bought the next day.

As it was our exam time we were given a week off before the torture started. That gave me a perfect opportunity to express my love for Urvashi. Only 1st years had classes in the morning and so even on this Tuesday, the 14th the lecture halls were going to be empty in the morning. With a couple of hundred bucks I arranged for the keys for the lecture hall. Once Urvashi left at 6 pm after our daily tuition, I rushed out to the city to get her a lot of chocolates. The library closed at 10 pm and once all the guys had left, I picked up my bag full of presents for my soon going to be girlfriend and headed straight to the lecture hall. I unlocked the door and entered the hall with utmost silence and started the computer. While it was loading windows I switched on the light focusing on the stage and started drawing on the black board. I drew two stick figures one wearing a blue jacket and one with a pink which appeared as if they were standing with their hands on each other's shoulders. By their side I wrote "Happy Valentine's Day Dear" in fancy cursive writing. Once the computer started, I uploaded the power point I had made especially for this day. When the projector started I could see the first slide on the big wide screen which read "The best thing that has ever happened to me!" and the following few slides had pictures of me and her and some of her alone. On the last slide I confessed about my love and wrote "For the rest of my life and not just today, will you be my valentine?"

By the time I finished all these preparations it was almost midnight. It was time to call her. My plan was to talk to her normally and invite her the next morning to the lecture hall and make my confession. So here I was, sitting on the 1st bench of the lecture hall, for a change, and dialling her number on my cell phone.

"The number you are trying to call is on another call, please hold the line or call again later."

Probably she was talking to one of her friends. I tried to explain myself.

After another two times of call waiting I started getting anxious. Considering she was one of the few girls in the hostel to have cell phones, may be one of her friends was using her phone to talk to their guys. That has to be the reason.

I started getting frustrated at the female with the recorded voice who told me that Urvashi's phone was still on call waiting. But I could do nothing but wait. After a painful, curious and anxious span of an hour and a half my phone rang in my pocket. A smile arouse on my lips and my eyes turned towards Urvashi's picture which was still on the wide screen. I made a gesture of a kiss looking at her picture and took my phone out. It was Suraj.

"Yes bro, did you call priyanka or not? Did you wish her already?" I asked.

"Yes I did. Forget that Himanshu. I want you to come back to the hostel immediately. Please don't ask why!" He said in hurry but a stern voice.

"Come on dude, I haven't spoken to her yet. I'll come back as soon as I speak to her." I replied.

"Himanshu, please listen to me. Just come back." He requested this time.

"Suraj what happened? Tell me." I asked.

"Her phone is on call waiting isn't it?" He asked.

"Yes it is but how the hell did you know? Suraj what is happening?" Now I was getting scared.

"I just heard that your Urvashi called up Sanil and asked him out, though I'm not sure about this news." Suraj explained.

"Dude, don't fuck with me. You know I really like her. Now don't mess up with my head." I requested Suraj with a quivering voice.

"Himanshu I'm not kidding with you. Just forget about the whole thing and come back to the hostel. Please." Suraj insisted.

I was shocked. I was as if my soul walked out on me. I couldn't even move an inch of my body. Air refused to enter my chest and my heart felt too tired to beat. I tried calling Urvashi again but her phone was still on call waiting. The next second Suraj called me again.

Dude, which lecture hall are you in? I'm here; let's go back to the hostel."

With a lot of difficulty the number '3' came out of my mouth. In a few seconds Suraj was there.

I was clearly in denial. No, Urvashi couldn't have done this to me. How could she?

"Himanshu, just stop thinking ok." He said while rubbing my drawings from the board. He next sat on the computer and deleted the presentation I had made for Urvashi. He came next to me, pulled my arm around his shoulder and dragged me out of the lecture hall. My eyes were filled with tears; they were rolling out one by one. Suraj tried to console me but those tears didn't stop. He walked me all the way to the hostel to his room. It was already past 2 in the morning. On stepping into the corridor I realized that all the lights were out except for Sanil's room. I could hear him talk and laugh every now and then.

"My roommate is sleeping in your room. You sleep in my room tonight ok." And he took me in.

My eyes still hadn't rested. They were still drenched with tears and so were my cheeks and neck along with my shirt. This was the first time I was so heartbroken. It was so painful I just could not compare.

Suraj passed me a towel and wiping my face, trying to control myself I asked "so how is priyanka?"

"Himanshu you don't think about anything now ok. Just lie down here and try to sleep ok." He said.

This way wetting Suraj's bed I just lay there, thinking about my fucked up fate, my pathetic loser heart. I could not sleep the whole night and even if by mistake I closed my eyes the picture of Sanil and Urvashi popped up in my head which made me even more awake. There were several times when I got up from the bed finding myself drenched in tears and sweat realizing Suraj was still wide awake studying for the exam. With the idea of giving him company and moving my mind of thoughts that were bothering me,

I asked Suraj to teach me something he was learning. But with every word of anatomy that came out of his mouth I was reminded of all those times I spent studying on the college stairs with Urvashi. I tried to control myself a lot but couldn't. I ended up bursting into tears again. I still remember, it was the worst night of my life.

"Himanshu, I'm going to sleep now, but if at all you need me for anything, just wake me up ok." Suraj said to me.

Just after the sun spread its light through the windows into the room, Suraj left his books and slept off, leaving me all by myself. Soon the clock hit 8 and Sandeep knocked his knuckles on the door. I realized I was still occupying Suraj's bed and he was sleeping on Sandeep's. I let him in and left the room myself. On my steps to my own room I found my roommate leaving for the library. And that was followed by a very long and lonely, tearful and painful day. My hands did not care to open the books; my eyes did not dare to close. I just lay on my bed the whole day doing nothing but feeling hurt and lonely.

The sleepless day turned into night and I didn't even get a hint. My roommate came back at midnight from the library all ready for the next day's exam and I was still stuck up here cursing my fate and life. Before I knew, the sun reached the midst of the sky and it was time for the exam already.

My body didn't want to move, I didn't want to go for the exam. But if I didn't, my dad would get to know, and clearly I had given him enough and more trouble. With a lot of difficulty I dragged myself out of the bed and reached the college. While I was taking my feet to the exam hall I found a lot of people sitting on those steps doing the last minute reading. Suddenly a frightening shock rested my heart beat to zero. The feeling I had 2 nights ago came back swiftly tingling every nerve of my body bringing pain worse than I could imagine. Sanil was sitting on the steps ahead of me, and right by his side was sitting that girl who screwed me over, holding his hands and listening to the anatomy he was blabbering. This was a worse impact than that night but somehow I controlled myself. I walked right past them and entered the exam hall before anyone else. In the next few minutes the exam hall was packed and question papers were distributed. To my bad luck Urvashi was in my vicinity from the chair I was allotted. It was not even 30 minutes past the start of the exam when I left the hall. I could hear a lot of mumbling and talks in the background when I stood up but I just couldn't bear the pain. I don't even remember reading the questions or writing anything but my roll number on the answer sheet. I came back to my room and cried and cried and cried. A few hours later my roommate walked in pushing the door open with a bang.

"What the fuck were you thinking Himanshu? What has got into you?" He was furious.

This was the first time I had heard him use that word. Before I could even say a word Suraj barged into the room and wacked me on the head. This was followed by a long and boring speech from the both of them together. There were a lot of times when they called me dumb, idiot, fool and a total nut crack. That night BD sat up with me through out and taught me physiology for the next day. This way at least my mind was diverted and once I was saturated I could get some sleep.

BD woke me up an hour before the exam and we made our walk to the exam hall together. Even though it was more than 2 hours that the exam had started and I had written everything I could, I did not dare to leave the hall this time as BD had threatened me with the idea of informing my parents regarding what grave I was leading myself into. Once the exam was over I walked out with Suraj and was picking up my bag when I heard a very familiar voice.

"Hey Himanshu how was the paper?"

This was the same voice I had heard in the blood bank few months ago. This was the same voice I fell head over heels for. And this was the same voice I was craving to hear two nights ago while her phone was busy.

I turned around to find her with a small smile on her face as if nothing had gone wrong. Very obviously her exam had gone well while I was doing everything I could to add 6 more months to the period of my 1ˢᵗ year.

"Tell me Himanshu, how was your exam?" Urvashi asked again.

Without my own intentions my feet turned around and brisk walked away. My eyes reddened again but I controlled the tears. What did she mean by "how was your paper Himanshu?" Doesn't she remember what had been happening for the last few months between me and her? And then she went and dumped my love and emotions into a trash can and proposed a douche bag that wasn't even half my height.

Yelling's and curses from BD and Suraj kept Urvashi out of my head for another night while BD struggled really hard to teach me biochemistry.

This last exam also followed the same pattern. Even though I was done writing everything I knew in less than an hour, I had to wait till the end because of BD and his threat. Like the previous day we left together and at the same spot again while picking up my bag I heard the same voice again.

Tapping me on my back she said "Himanshu what is wrong with you? Why aren't you talking to me? You walked away yesterday and you didn't even respond to any of my messages or calls. What is up with you?"

"What is wrong with me? What do you mean what is wrong with me? And I'm so surprised that you even got time to message or call me. Isn't Sanil giving you enough time? And why did you call me anyways? To know how pathetic I am these days because of you or how I'm screwing up my life all thanks to you? What do you want to know Urvashi? Yes I'm fucking up my exams and you do know the reason don't you? Tell me Urvashi? Don't you know why I'm so fucked up?"

"Himanshu I was just trying to . . ."

"Trying to what Urvashi? Trying to what? First you screw me over and now what are you trying to do here? What do you expect from me?"

"Nothing Himanshu, I was just . . ."

By now tears were over flowing on her red cheeks and she was gasping for breath. A short distance away I could see Sanil standing and witnessing the entire scene but for some reason he didn't dare to step in and interrupt. So I continued.

"Whatever it is Urvashi, you screwed me over, you acted like a fucking bitch and I'm the one who is suffering because of you. Can you even justify what you did to me? Tell me Urvashi."

By now her face was flooded with tears and I found her running away from me. The crowd was stunned for I had spoken or rather screamed really loud at her. Everyone was staring at me but I cared less. I picked up my bag gestured to BD that I was leaving and left.

Days went by as if the sun didn't even rise up. My schedule of going to class, skipping lunch, getting back to the hostel was the common thing along with occasional tears that my eyes let out every now and then. Even after yelling at her and somewhat taking my frustration out, I was still a mess, for the fact I was considering to apologize to her for being rude in front of so many people, but BD's strong NO's kept me from doing that. Everyday BD or Suraj would come to me and try to convince me to move on but I was still stuck with the fact that she can't be so cruel. I kept digging my thoughts, trying to find a fault in myself. It had to be my bad. Because according to me she was this flawless beautiful angel who, probably by mistake, shot an arrow right through my heart. It was very difficult to find a reason to why she did this to me. She told me that she loved me, that she cared for me. She spent time with me more than anybody else. So it had to be something that I did. So the next day in class I came up with the idea of asking the question to her directly.

Most of the students were still trying to find seats wandering between the rows when BD walked in the classroom. I waved my hand towards him, and he realized I wanted him there. I started pouring my thoughts out as soon as he parked himself on the seat next to me.

"I'm going to ask her why she did this to me!" I declared.

"Are you crazy? You are not doing anything like that Himanshu! Suraj!!" while waving his hand out to him he screamed "come here fast, it's an emergency."

"What happened?" Suraj asked.

"This idiot wants to ask Urvashi why she did this to him!" BD explained.

"Oh my God, you have to be out of your mind to do such a thing. No way dude, we won't let you do anything of that sort." Suraj said.

"What's the big deal? I'm just going to ask her a question and she is going to reply, and I'll walk away, as simple as that." I justified.

"Yeah right, are you really going to stop at that?" BD asked.

"Hmmm, maybe one or two more questions, but after that I'll stop for sure." I replied.

"Himanshu, if you do it, I am never talking to you again!" Suraj said.

"Neither am I!" BD joined him.

"Guys, I'm not falling for that ok. I'm going to do it now!" I exclaimed.

I stood up from my seat and started browsing for Urvashi. Suddenly I heard the latch of the class room door close and pin drop silence following that. It was a half bald man, probably in his early 40's, in a jeans and a casual shirt. Even though he did not appear at all like a professor, he introduced himself as the new assistant professor of physiology who was going to teach us "Reproductive system"!

"Good morning, boys and beautiful girls!" He wished everyone.

And everyone had a "who the fuck is he?" expression on their faces.

Sticking the mic closer to his mouth he barked again.

"Most of you know me already but for the sake of the dumb boys and these pretty eyes (pointing at the girls), he said "I'm Dr Spandan, Assistant professor of physiology, and I'm going to enlighten you with the knowledge of the reproduction process, even though most of you don't need a class on the topic, and some of you have practiced it too."

This followed a more silent silence because none of us were used to such straight forward statements. The boys liked him for sure, just for the fact that he spoke about sex, even indirectly. And he started with his class.

His first slide popped up and all of us literally stopped breathing. It had two pictures, one of a guy with his shlong and the other was a girl with her pom pom. I don't need to tell you how shocked we all were when this happened.

Pointing at the pictures he said "Today we are going to learn about this, but before this I'm going to take some time to introduce myself properly, and then followed by your introduction. Wait, do we really need that? We'll just skip through that and proceed to re-enlightening of what you guys know already. Ok so once again I am Dr Spandan, I did my UG from Karnataka university college, I did PG from Maharashtra university, I have published 14 papers in all, 6 during UG and the rest during PG and ever since, I've been interested in research work.

But above all of these, my best achievement is the fact that I discovered something. After so many years of hard work, I finally did something that was worth the world to know about. And that is . . ."

And the next slide read.

"Indian scientist discovers gold in human body fluid"

And the next line in small fonts read—"Gold in human semen."

Every single person in the room was silent. We just did not know how to respond to that. Few of us were thinking of it as a normal thing for a professor to do, and some of them just didn't get it or they didn't care.

For a very quiet response from the crowd he spoke again "For those who did not understand, I discovered traces of gold in a human fluid which most of us dispose of almost every other day"

The class was yet again stunned with blank faces and sealed lips. We still didn't know how to react.

This time, in an annoyed tone, he said "Maybe you don't appreciate this but others have!"

Flipping on to the next slide he blabbered some names and the comments and statements those great people had made on Dr. Spandan's discovery. Most of us still kept quiet and few mumbled some words to the dummies parked next to them. But the last comment from some film director got our attention.

"Gold in semen? I always knew these women were gold suckers!"

This was the threshold cut off for all of us boys. We all went crazy and started banging the desks just like the chimpanzees do on their chests. We were wooing for him and the girls were just embarrassed except for one. Just one girl, somewhere from the 1st benches turned around giggling the second "gold sucker" travelled to our ears. Us boys stopped and gazed at her for a while till she realized it was the dumbest thing to do, and then we all started laughing at her.

Even that evening in the boy's hostel, discussion on the same topic continued.

"I'm sure that guy is gay, or else why is he so interested in human semen?" Sunil expressed his thought.

"Dude that girl, Dipika has such humongous boobs; I want to name her Boobster." Sanil added to the conversation.

"That is a good one." Sunil gave his approval.

"Dude I'm sure she'll fuck even for a penny!" Sanil replied.

"She will or she did?" Winking at us Rajesh made this statement and left the room.

But the thought of me messing things up with Urvashi never left my mind. I knew I was in a complete mess. First of all I had lost the girl I really thought things were going to work out with, and then I screwed up my exams. But the thought that Urvashi ditched me was due to my bad kept torturing my mind. I could not have called her and asked because BD had deleted her number from my phone. I was helpless and lonely.

And soon "The funniest moments of my life part II" was released. It was the same tension in the class. No single person was moving their lips or hearts. Fingers were crossed and eyes were wide open waiting for the dreadful result. I wouldn't tell you what the view was like, but I can sure tell you that I was one amongst the top comedians in part II. My eyes were almost filled with tears but I couldn't have let them out. On the far corner of the hall I could see, with my red wet eyes, the joy between Urvashi and Sanil, for both of them had passed. And that made me feel more terrible. Not that I wanted them to fail, but it should have been me in place of that dwarf celebrating with her.

In the next few days I learned that I had made a hat trick. I had failed all three subjects. And I was the only one in the whole batch to do so. Most of them had at least passed in one out of three. This brought me into the notice of a lot more people, especially the professors. And soon a notice came which invited all the students who had failed in more than one subject to meet the HOD's of the respective departments.

At the end of the day, while I was walking out of the lecture hall preparing myself and thinking of any possible excuses for the HOD's, someone tapped me on my shoulder from behind.

My pupils widened the second I turned around; I turned to stone and couldn't move for it was Urvashi standing right in front of me.

"Himanshu I need to talk to you, do you mind?" She said in a harsh and commanding tone.

"Sure" I squeaked.

Most of the students were just outside the hall when she ordered me to sit down. My ass hadn't even touched the cushion and she had started already.

"What is wrong with you? Are you trying to tell the whole world how madly and deeply you are in love with me? Or how dumb you are to screw up things for me? And how stupid of you to think that I am going to fall for you! Seriously Himanshu, you really think any girl here would date you? You must be out of your mind to feel that way. Sanil is so much better than you in every possible way. Himanshu you are just making things difficult for me and if you think that . . ."

Realizing that tears were flowing like a river through my eyes, BD had come in to interrupt Urvashi.

"Himanshu let's go! And Urvashi please leave him alone." BD said pulling me out of the seat.

"Ask him to leave me alone!" Urvashi screamed at our backs.

Even though the crowd had now accumulated around the door listening to every word that stuck my heart like an arrow, BD made way and carried me out. We skipped the meeting with the HOD's and he took me back to the hostel. BD realized my pitiful state and decided to leave me alone in my room, leaving me with the loneliness I needed at that point of time. I just occupied my small bed wetting the sheets like I had been doing for the past many days when a knock on the door broke my continuous stream of tears.

"Who is it?" I asked.

"It's Karan, just want to talk to you for a while." came the response.

He was a good friend but what did he want from me? In a state of confusion I let the door swing.

He walked in and we both placed ourselves on the two beds opposite to each other.

"So you want to talk about it?" Karan asked.

"About what?" I asked.

"About what has been happening with you and that bitch?" He replied.

In that moment I wished I could just slap that guy but wasn't he correct. Soon I let my heart door open with those of my eyes and told him about how we started, how things were going, about 14th February and how things turned around. I told him everything.

"Listen Himanshu, these kinds of things happen in life. I have gone through an incidence myself, in fact two. I'm not saying that all of them are the same but most of them are. So you have got to be careful. You have to be honest and think for your own about what your real priorities are. Do you think the expectations your parents have of you are less important than whoever this girl is? No Himanshu! Girls will come and go but you can't hold on to them with such strong feelings. The sooner you get over this, the better it will be for you. Get over her, go hunt for someone else. I'm sure she isn't the only pretty girl in your batch, is she? And please don't get attached to them like you did with Urvashi ok. You are so young. You don't need to get into a commitment right away, do you? Go around with people, have fun and use your opportunities to the maximum, if you know what I mean."

All I could do was nod to everything he was saying. And he continued to tell me how I should be flirting around with girls and not settle down with a disappointed heart. He even offered me tips on how to get girls. But my mind was still stuck with only one face. I was being a stubborn retard. But I didn't know what else to do.

While Karan continued with his class on how to score, someone yelled from outside the room "Himanshu you've got a call!"

I wiped my face and ran out into the corridor to pick up the ringing phone. And even before I could keep the phone to my ears I could hear words that were not so pleasant to hear.

"All you had to do was to study a little bit and pass. I never asked you to get a rank or even first class. All you had to do was pass the exams and you couldn't do that. What am I supposed to do now? I expected so much from you Himanshu, but you have completely disappointed me. First your brother and now you too! Himanshu I don't have a lot of years left, only god knows when he is going to call me up. But the time I have left here, I want to see my children stand up on their feet. Is that too much to ask?"

With that question my Dad took a long pause. I was not sure if he wanted me to respond to his question, but even if he did want me to, I didn't know what to reply. I was ashamed of myself. I started to realize things and finally some sense started seeping into my brains. How could I do this to myself? How could I let her affect me so much? How could she be more important than my parents? I just realized how much of an idiot I was.

"Himanshu I'm not going to say anything more to you. Maybe I have been harsh with you but I was only doing my job. If you can't realize that then there is nothing more that I can do. Hope you understand what I am trying to say and find your lost path soon. And remember, if there is anything bothering you, or you need to share, your father is going to be there for you!"

I heard the phone take its place down. That phone call, that small talk from my father did something to me. I just realized that I was being the dumbest guy ever on this earth. It was not worth it. The bitch wasn't worth it. For the first time I called her a bitch myself and it didn't bother me. If she wants to go on with a heavy headed dwarf that is her choice, that doesn't mean I sit here alone waiting for her to come back. It's her loss, not mine!

Chapter Eleven

"I'M SO PROUD OF YOU MY SON"

And just like that I was over Urvashi. But I had made some more decisions. What happened between me and Urvashi wasn't going to happen again, for it wasn't really worth it. My brother had once told me never to run behind girls who don't give you enough importance and those who do would run behind you. I had now started to incorporate that advice into my life. I was going to score more for sure, and those girls were going to get a lot of me, but definitely no feelings. But now I had to face a bigger problem for myself. Sitting around wetting my eyes was very easy of a job, but now I had to make up for all the time I had lost for my studies. The last time I opened my books were when I was teaching that bitch. And I had wasted over 2 months doing nothing but crying over stupid things my life had no place for. Now it was time to sit down and study. I wasn't sure if I could do it. I literally didn't know anything about any subject. I knew I had to struggle a lot in the next couple of months.

A theory exam was scheduled in another 2 days and this was the best way to find out if I could cope up with the stress and turn back on my path correctly and quickly. It was a class test on the topic 'abdomen' by the anatomy department. It was supposed to be an easier exam as the colour queen had given us 16 questions in advance and only 6 of them were going be asked. And so, with just 24 hours for the test to start I sat down with my anatomy book when BD walked in with a sleep deprived 'I'm fucked for tomorrow's exam' face into the room.

"What happened to you BD?" I expressed my concern.

"Dude I haven't slept in a while, and I was preparing for the head and neck spotters which is next week. I didn't even study a word for the test tomorrow. I'm going to fail for sure." He replied.

"You want to sit down and study with me?" I offered.

"I'm very sleepy Himanshu, don't think I . . . wait a second. You are studying for tomorrow's test?" His sleepless face had a surprised look now.

"Yup!" I replied with a smile.

"What happened to you? I mean how did this miracle happen?" Now he was taunting me.

"Are you going to shut up or should I kick your butt?" I asked politely.

"Fine fine, you study, I'm going to sleep!" BD replied.

"Sleep my ass. I'm going to teach you for tomorrow's exam and you better sit and listen or else the consequences would be painful." I warned him.

"Ok. But I will not guarantee if I can escape my sleep." He agreed.

"We'll see."

And I started teaching him anatomy of abdomen, sitting face to face on either of the beds. Every now and then BD would start dozing off to which I would either scream or whack him with a belt which was lying next to me. This way we sat up for about 6 hours and finished 9 out of 16 questions. This was when we realized that both of us were too sleepy to study anymore. I kept the book down to sleep and BD dozed off the next second.

The test was the best thing that happened to me after I got over Urvashi. 6 questions were asked in the exam out of which 5 of them were from the 9 questions that we had studied. BD gave me a smile and I caught his eyes.

We both knew we were going to pass. In the next 3 days our papers were corrected and I scored the 3rd highest and BD the 4th highest in the class. My will got a boost and I was all set to study hard for the head and neck spotters for next week. This was the first sign that moving on was a better thing to do than to sit down and cry.

We were a batch of hundred and there were 25 spotters. Roll numbers were called in a sequence and the test was held in 4 different batches. The 'D' batch was called first, then 'A' then 'B' and then in the end my batch. In the whole anatomy, head and neck was considered the toughest as it had the tiniest of structures and so many in numbers. So to make it easier, some people decided to take their phones and make the test easier by cheating. Sunil was in 'D' batch and got done with the spotters first and as soon as it was over for him he typed in all the spotters and texted it to Sanil. Now it would have been very easy for him to pass if he hadn't done a stupid thing. He called in all the people around him and blurted out the answers. It was a nice thing for the boys but the loud speakers were a part of the group too, I meant the girls. The 'A' batch went in next. Nobody said anything during the exam. The test went on with a pin drop silence. But at the end of the exam some of those girls suddenly felt guilty. Their test went well but their conscience did not let them keep shut. They went to the HOD and told her that they were informed about the spotters before the exam by a student. Immediately KKK with her troop came to the classroom where we all were waiting to be called in next. All of our bags and bodies were checked. Few people were caught with their phones including Sanil. That idiot hadn't even deleted the text from Sunil which had all the answers. And so he had to face some terrible consequences. The test was cancelled immediately and both of them were called to the principal's office. Upon reaching the office Sanil was questioned about his visit to the nearby beach with Urvashi. Now this came as a surprise to all of us. Apparently they were spotted on the weekend, holding hands together at the beach by some doctor who had informed the happening to the principal. This meant only one thing. Sanil got fucked.

Urvashi and Sanil were both suspended till further orders. It sure did give me a feeling of joy within but I wasn't concerned much now. Their parents were called to meet the disciplinary committee. They both were called by the principal a number of times and questioned again and again. Their life was in a mess for a small little mistake.

On the other hand I was moving on quite well, interacting more with friends and seniors and studying everyday preparing for the final exams that were only a month away.

After a terrible, tiring and exhausting torture with books for a month, the exams were finally over and I was home. I was happy for the fact that my exams went well. But I had told otherwise to my parents as I wanted them to get a surprise when I passed with good marks, so even when I reached home there wasn't a proper response from them. It was just a daily routine that was going on in the house, nothing special for me. Dad would leave for hospital as soon as he would get ready and mom would spend most of her time in the kitchen. And I used to spend most of the time on the computer. It was very difficult to stop myself from telling them that my exam was good and that I will pass. That way I could also have reduced the attitude that I was getting from them. But their expressions when they find out that I passed would be priceless. And I wanted to see that myself.

Few days later dad came in the afternoon much before lunch time and screamed calling me to the hall. This was an odd time for him to come back; moreover it was a working day. When I stepped into the hall I saw dad standing up straight with a blank face and mom standing right behind him with a small grin on her face. I was confused. I had no idea what was happening.

As I approached closer to my dad, he quickly took few steps towards me, hugged me and exclaimed "I'm so proud of you my son!"

I was shocked. I kept asking myself what made dad say that. What did you do Himanshu?

"You ranked second in class and you told us that your exam was bad?" My mom said tapping my cheeks.

"What the . . . who told you that? I did not rank second in class. That is impossible." I was in denial.

"Don't lie to me son, I got a call from the principal's office and they told me that roll number 71, that's you, ranked second in class. That was the only reason they called, because my son ranked 2nd in class. I'm going to tell all of my friends." Dad explained.

"Dad that's not possible. I might have passed, maybe first class, but 2nd rank, definitely not. Let me check on the net." I replied.

I rushed into my room and clicked on the internet explorer, and my homepage of orkut opened up. There were many new scraps to check and so I clicked on them. My scrap book was scribbled all over with congrats for the 2nd rank from most of my batch mates. How was that possible? My papers were not that good. I was sure to pass but not a rank. I was so shocked and confused I decided to call the college.

I gave in my roll number and she said "2nd rank, distinction in all 3 subjects." I almost dropped the phone from my hands. I asked her to check again but she declared the same result. Now I started to think if the paper was so bad for the others that I scored a rank. But it was not possible. It could have never happened. Getting the 2nd rank in class? Not even in my dreams.

I told the same thing to dad but he wasn't ready to listen to me. Now I was scared. What if the results got switched with someone else and I didn't even clear the exam. So I called Karan to check out the list of students who had failed. He called me back after an hour denying my name in the failed student's list. Now I was happy for at least one thing that I did not fail. Everything convinced me that I ranked 2nd but I wasn't just ready to accept it. But it did turn out to be a good thing for me. I got a new phone and a laptop. Mom and dad were happy.

The next few days at home were the best I could have. The best food I've ever had, all the freedom I ever wanted. Life was blissful but soon I had to get back to college for 2nd year. I had now passed the most difficult exam of my career and was ready to face new books, professors and for the first time, patients.

Chapter Twelve

"WHY THE LEFT BREAST?"

We had 4 subjects for the second year and we all thought it would be much more difficult to cope up along with clinics and more practical classes that were included. But one thing that was easier this time was getting back to the hostel. We knew who we were going to find in our rooms, our understanding roommates. And as soon as we got back to the rooms the gossips started. Everyone wanted to find out how the other's holidays were. But when Suraj walked into my room he asked just one question. How are you doing now Himanshu?

"What do you mean by how he is doing? This bloody bugger ranked 2nd in the freaking class and you are asking him how he is doing? I feel you have started to lose your brains now." BD almost screamed.

"I still can't believe it guys. There has to be a mistake. There is no freaking way that I would score more than Suraj and many others in the class." I responded.

And so we decided to go to the exam control division to sort things out the next day. But we had a long schedule to attend before we could do that. We had five hours of clinics scheduled for the next day and then pathology practical class in the afternoon. We were divided into two halves and the 2nd half in which I belonged was posted in general surgery first, the subject I liked, even though I didn't know much about it yet. But as I was excited, I was one among the first few students to reach the department of general surgery the next day. As I entered class I decided to catch a seat at the back. I didn't want to be the first to be asked a question and make a fool out of myself. I sat a little behind the ex-girl of my dreams who was playing with his little boy toy, but it didn't bother me at all. Soon the class was filled by students and even sooner the brigadier walked in. Now when we heard the name 'Brigadier Dr. Philip' we pictured him to be this tall, muscular dark man with a big moustache and an awesome personality. But what walked in instead looked more like a retired constable. He was short about 5'6 feet with thick framed glasses. He was dark alright but wasn't built at all. He had a round tummy which was pretty much obvious. He did have a moustache but it barely had much hair on it. The only thing which made him look like a brigadier or rather sound like one was his voice.

He came in, closed the door behind him and in his heavy bold voice said "hello doctors" and even the dumbasses that never paid attention in class turned upright straight and started listening to him.

"You all have just passed your first year. Congratulations to all of you. But don't think that it is going to be the same. Everything is going to be different from now on. We are going to expose you to the practical application of being a doctor. We are going to expose you to the patients."

With that short speech he took a pause and then started again with the basics of history taking. He taught us how the bio data including name, age, gender, occupation and the address of the patient might help us reach a diagnosis. And then he explained how to extract the history from the patient and the general examination. At the end of the class we were asked to go take up a case and write down a proper history of the patient's illness, come back in an hour and present it to him. So we all headed towards the wards to take up a case.

In an hour we were all back to the class, few of us from the wards, and most of the others from the canteen who had found time to meet their girls. When we walked in the brigadier was already waiting for us, sitting on the chair with his one leg over the other, gripping his hands together as if he was planning a strategy on how to go behind enemy lines. We all came in quickly and took our seats. We had decided to put Shalini forward to present the case as she was the topper of the class. And with the case presentation she started.

Name—Laxmi Nair

Age—43 years

Gender—Female

Occupation—House wife

Address—Allepy

At the end of this the brigadier got up and without him commanding there was a pin drop silence in the class. With his heavy voice he started again.

"This is not how you present a case. It is not a prerequisite form that you have filled and reading out to me. You should have a command over the language and present it like a story that is pleasant to hear. People should listen to it like a fairy tale and understand every bit of it giving all of their concentration. They should be immersed in the story and at the end every single student who has heard the case should be able to reach a diagnosis. I will take a class again tomorrow and one of you is going to present this same case again but like a story. Understood?"

With perfect coordination we all nodded yes.

"Am I understood?" He commanded raising his voice.

And we all said in a chorus "Yes sir" as if we were scouts standing in the sun ready to hike a mile on his command.

Next we all headed to the mess hall for lunch and after a full tummy meal and a lot of disagreeing congratulations received from the seniors for my rank we headed to the pathology department. It was a comparatively smaller room as the class was only for 30 students. We took our seats and soon a fat dark lady walked in who seemed to cross my memory vaguely.

"Oh shit, she is the same lazy fatty who denied giving me extra papers in my anatomy exam." I whispered to Suraj sitting next to me.

During the anatomy paper, which was my strongest subject, I had written so much and asked for so many answer sheets that this professor, who was in charge of the additional sheets, was pissed with me as she had to walk her fat ass to me every now and then. I was sure she was going to remember me and take her revenge.

"Good afternoon kids. Let us get done with your attendance and then we will start off with the basics of histopathology" and she opened the register for attendance.

"So we seem to have amongst ourselves a bright student of the lot who did not stop to pen down every little detail he could for his exams. So tell me Himanshu, was writing so much in your anatomy paper help you in anyway?"

"Fuck" was the only word that came out of my mouth in whispers for the fact that she had identified me. But my 2nd rank was still with me and I proudly stood up and with over flowing confidence said "Yes Ma'am, it did get me 2nd rank"

"You jerk. So you did rank 2nd didn't you?" asked Suraj next to me in a low but annoyed and angry tone.

"No dude I was just trying to . . ."

"So Mr 2nd rank, tell me what are the principles of a microscope?" Dr Bindiya asked me.

I was as blank as the empty page of the notebook in front of me.

"How does a muscle look like under the microscope?" Her questions continued.

I still kept mum.

"Awww the rank holder doesn't know even the basics? It is so disappointing." She said in a teasing voice.

I was still quiet and was thinking what I did so wrong for her to pick on me.

"Don't try to be smart in my class ok. Sit down quietly and listen to the class." She said angrily.

What the fuck? Did I interrupt her? Did I insult her or back answer? Then why was she so annoyed with me? I had many angry thoughts in my mind but all I could do was shut up and sit down.

She started the projector and the class went on.

And Suraj sitting next to me had a grin on his face for Bindiya mam was going to take classes for us the whole month and that meant that I was going to get screwed for the entire month.

Once the class was over I picked up BD from the microbiology department and we went straight to the exam control division. Suraj tagged along with us as he was sure I couldn't have out casted him in exams. We met the computer guy who enters marks in the system and found out that he couldn't have made a mistake as he was only given a list to enter. But when we checked out that list we found Rakhi, the roll number next to me, scored only a 1st class which was a little difficult to believe as she was one of the top scorers for most of the semester exams. So we requested the head of the exam control division to look into the matter. With a disapproving smile he said he will do so. We waited there for some time when he came back to us and declared that there was some mistake and my marks were swapped with those of Rakhi. I finally took a sigh of relief and proudly told BD that I was right and couldn't have scored a rank. Suraj standing next to us had an even bigger smile for pretty obvious reason.

On the way back BD advised me to take the mic in class the next day before the teacher arrives and give away the rank to her much deserved owner and I agreed with a nod even though it wouldn't have been necessary as we were sure that the news would reach the girl's hostel much before we announce it as Suraj had started dating a girl from the same batch.

The next day we were all ready with the same case to face the brigadier again. He needed a story out of the case and so we picked on the right person for the case presentation, Sheetal. Her dad was a writer and so she had the instincts of that to pen down the case in a story format. He walked in with his tummy wobbling and raised his hand in a gesture which meant to start the presentation. And so Sheetal started.

Once upon a time there was a patient named Laxmi Nair that had complaints of a swelling in the . . .

"What is this?" The Brigadier interrupted.

"Sir you wanted it to be like a story so I was . . ."

"Is this some kind of a joke to all of you? A case presentation is the most important thing for a student in MBBS as it is that which is going to get you through the exams. You bunch of buffoons don't understand anything or should I presume that you all are just not interested?" The Brigadier was furious.

"No sir it's not . . ." Sheetal tried to explain.

"Don't utter a word young lady. All of you follow me to my cabin. Attend the clinics with me and I will tell you how to take a case." The Brigadier calmed down.

He ordered us to split up and go to three different rooms and attend the clinics with those different doctors who were there. And unfortunately I fell into the group that followed the brigadier into his room.

He took his chair and we gathered behind him while he ordered the secretary to send in the next patient. Soon a couple walked into the room and took the chairs opposite the brigadier.

"Tell me lady, what is your problem?"

It sounded more like he was interrogating her instead of taking a history.

With much hesitation she murmured that she felt a swelling in her left breast accidentally. After elaborating some more history the brigadier asked her to sit on the bed behind the curtain. Like little puppets we followed him behind the curtain where he was going to examine the case. The patient was asked to take her blouse off and with a lot of hesitation she did. Some of the guys just dropped their jaws and I reasoned it to be the 1st chance for them to look at a real breast. It wasn't much surprising for me as I had seen some before, and they were better. After touching her breast here and there he made a couple of girls to examine the case and went back to his chair. He then advised the husband that she needed a small surgery to take out the lump and it will all be fine. Once the patient reasoned and understood the need for surgery they left the room and the brigadier presented the case to us in its correct way. We all understood and nodded in agreement when the next case came in. Coincidentally the next patient's problem was the same as the 1st ones. She too had a lump in her left breast. The same following happened and the patient was advised about surgery and sent off. After 3 hours of standing with him in the clinic we had witnessed many cases of breast lumps, hernias and many more. Towards the end when it was time for us to leave one of our young ladies dared to ask a question.

"Sir we have seen four cases of breast lumps today and all of them were on the left breast. Why is it that it is more common on the left side than right?" Shalini asked.

We were all concentrating with our ears wide open for a very technical and scientific answer from the brigadier.

"My dear doctor, I don't have a documented explanation to that but it is probably because most of the men are right handed." The Brigadier explained.

Most of the girls were confused with the answer but I had immediately gone back to the imagination of my experiences and realized what he meant. Controlling our laughter and hiding my evil grin we all left the clinic for lunch.

While we were having lunch we came up with a plan of bunking class and watching a movie. At first I was a little hesitant for I had had been into enough and more trouble since the beginning of the course. Two of us who were not coming for the movie, Suraj and Suman, took responsibility of giving us proxy in the class. With that idea and the compulsive forces of my buddies I agreed for the plan. But I had to go to class any ways to give away my 2nd rank to Rakhi even though I preferred keeping it as it was getting me a lot of attention from the first years that had joined recently, especially the girls.

So after lunch I went straight to class, hopped on to the stage and took the mic as more than half the students had already reached. Very soon I was done with the followings and as such there was not much of a response from the crowd as we knew that most of them would have been informed about the news beforehand. BD and 3 others were standing by the Dias waiting for me to finish so we could head out for the movie. So I told Akarsh, who had just entered the class, to give me proxy and started my feet for the lift.

"Himanshu come on, we'll take the stairs. It'll be faster." BD suggested.

"No dude. If I take stairs I'll be all sweaty. I'm going to wait for the lift. You guys can go for the stairs if you want to." I replied.

"Fine we'll see you near the bus stop." BD replied.

And so like a dumbass I stood there waiting for the lift to arrive and my friends started running down the stairs. Soon the lift door opened while I was looking out the window.

"What are you doing here Himanshu?" It was Dr. C.G. Nayar.

119

"Hmmm, noth . . . nothing ma'am." I was surprised.

"Are you not supposed to be in class?" She asked again.

"Ma'am I was heading to the class only." I replied.

"How come you were waiting here then? Are you waiting here for some girl?" She doubted me now.

"No no no ma'am. I had taken the stairs so was just catching my breath before I go more." I tried to give an excuse.

"But I don't see you panting." Now she was getting suspicious.

"Ummm I was till now ma'am. Now I'm feeling fine. Shall we go to the class ma'am?" I asked her.

She hummed in a disagreeing manner and started in front of me. We entered the class together and I had to take the seat in the front benches. Like always she started off with the attendance. Roll no 1, present ma'am, 2, present ma'am, 3, yes ma'am . . . .

70 present ma'am, 71 (three people in chorus) present ma'am!

She looked up to the crowd and took off her glasses. I was solely standing there like a dumbass while Akarsh and Suman who had both tried to give me proxy, quickly sat down. She stared at me in anger and then started with absurd convictions.

"So Mr. Himanshu first you wait outside my class for your girlfriends and then you have more friends inside who give you proxy. You don't study anything and try to spread your charm to everyone around. Is this how you are going to become a doctor? Why do you do these things? All I'm asking you is to be sincere with your studies. If you would have missed your class and if in the exam this question came then you will regret bunking this class won't you?"

I nodded in agreement even though I had no idea how she was co-relating the whole incident.

"You are like my own son; won't you listen to your mother? I am like your mother am I not?"

The clouds of her motherly love had gathered again and I had no option to nod my head up and down. While I was doing that I heard a phone ring in the back ground. Immediately following that there was some mumbling in the crowd, some sounds of quick hand motions and the ring tone hit volume zero. Suddenly the mother of all the children disappeared and she was back to her bitchy self.

"Whose phone was that? Stand up and hand over the phone to me." She screamed into the mic.

Fortunately the ringing phone's owner wasn't so dumb to do so. And with no response from the crowd she started off again.

"We care for you. You are all like my children and that is why I ask you to not have mobile phones in the campus. They are very dangerous. They affect your studies so much. And you my dear ones don't understand. Now please stand up and give the phone to me my child."

The mother India inside of her had woken up yet again. But there was still no response from anyone in the crowd. Observing her attention divert from myself to the class I quietly sat down as I didn't want to get screwed for being given proxy for.

Now she started to get angry, her motherly love started vanishing again and the bitchy anger was visible in her eyes.

"Fine, if you decide not to be good and keep your phone, do so. I am going to inform the principal about this incident. And then you will all see what happens."

No one even moved an inch from the crowd.

Getting more annoyed and angry she said "I'm going to inform the principal right now and I will check each and every one of you personally. And if found with a phone you will be punished."

We all still remained mum.

She immediately took her phone out and called the principal. In less than 15 minutes the principal arrived with a bunch of his clowns, as in members of disciplinary committee and formed two teams, one each for the two genders. Before making any further moves he announced "If any one of you is found with a phone, you will be suspended and fined heavily. So if someone does have a phone, this is the time to hand it over to me." After a span of two minutes without a response from the students he gestured to his team to start the checking and personally joined one of the crews.

I being on the front benches was called first. I had quickly hidden my phone under my seat cushion as putting it in my undies would be very obvious at such close distance from the friskers. I walked towards them and Rakesh Pai snatched away my bag and started searching inside out while our principal personally felt both the pockets on my pants on the front and the back and declared that I'm clean. There was only one pen and one notebook in my bag which came as a surprise to the principal.

"Are you an MBBS student or an engineering student?" He asked while all others in the back laughed at the expression.

In one of the smaller packets Rakesh Pai found my I-pod to which he burst out of joy and exclaimed "I found it!"

"So you were the one whose phone rang in class?" The principal asked me while the rest of the crowd took a sigh thinking there would be no further checking.

"No sir." I replied.

"So whose phone are you carrying in your bag?" He questioned examining my I-pod in his hand.

"That is not a phone to begin with sir." I replied.

"What? Let me see. What is this? I-pod?" The Principal asked inspecting the IPod in his hand.

"It is a music player sir. They can watch dirty videos also in this sir. I also have one at home." Rakesh Pai confessed with a smile.

I wished I could have asked if dirty videos were what he watches on his I-pod but I kept quiet.

"So is that what you do on this i-po whatever?" The principal asked me.

"No sir. There are no videos in the I-pod." I answered.

"Why didn't you hand it over to me when I asked for it?" He asked again.

"Sir you asked for phones, and I didn't have one here." I replied.

"So you have one back at home?" He asked.

"Yes sir I do." I agreed.

"Rakesh check his hostel room also and get me his phone." The Principal ordered Rakesh.

"No sir I don't have one in the hostel." I explained.

"You just said that you do." Now the Principal was confused.

"I said I have one at home. I didn't say I have one in the hostel." I tried to reason.

"Keep that electronic thing with you Rakesh. We will impose fine on him for having this in class. Call the next student." He told Rakesh.

"Sir but I don't have a . . ."

"Leave the class room now!" The Principal ordered.

Within few minutes the space just outside lecture hall started filling with students and the principal's bag with mobile phones. Many of the guys had put their phones in their under wears because that was one place the principal wouldn't dare to check. Similarly some of the girls grew their boob sizes but only one side. And those who couldn't hide them well, or had negligible assets were caught. A list was made of all the students who were caught with electronic devices and was put up on the notice board. We were all fined 5,000 Rs. for doing the misconduct. Unlike many others who had their eyes wet because of the notice, I on the other hand was used to seeing my name on the notice board so often and it didn't bother me. What bothered me more was the inter college dance competition that was due in 2 weeks and that I was made a part of the college dance group along with the seniors.

Chapter Thirteen

"A JOB WELL DONE"

All sweaty and panting for breath, everyone was totally tired after a hectic dance practice for two straight hours in the mess hall. But I was still at my maximum energy level and was still shouting at people for making the mistakes. Our dance group was formed by all the batches of MBBS but I was the only one from my batch. Seniors and super seniors would follow my commands like puppets. This was the only time when I could yell at those seniors and they could not say even a word back to me. I loved being the dance leader. While I was helping Sijith with one of his steps, Karan went to the speakers and increased the volume after glancing at his phone. Music was now so loud that even the people on the third floor could hear the music. From the partially open door of the mess I could see some people running into the gym. They banged on the gym door; the door swiftly swung open and was locked within a blink of an eye. I didn't understand what was happening and so I walked towards the gym to find out.

"Where are you going Himanshu?" Sijith inquired from behind.

"I just wanted to check out what was . . ."

Reducing the volume of the music Karan asked "Hey guys, let us stop the dance practice. We did enough for today, didn't we?

All of the guys agreed and seemed happy. While everyone was walking out Karan came up to me and said "Go to your room and stay there."

"Ok" I said in a confused gesture but the dance practice was now over and if I had raised my voice I would have been beaten down to red meat. So I quietly followed his order.

On my way back to the room I heard a loud scream. I realized that it had come from the gym. I quickly turned around ready to make a sprint to investigate what was happening. As I did so I realized Karan was standing just ahead of me, already changed, holding a bag on his shoulders heading out to the library.

"What did I tell you Himanshu? It is for your own good. Now go back to your room!" He ordered me this time.

And so I turned around again and started walking back to my room. I did hear a couple more screams but I ignored and kept walking. I reached my corridor to find it insanely quiet and abandoned. All the rooms were unlit as if everyone had slept off. I reached my door and knocked. The door unlocked and a whisper asked me to come in quickly.

"What happened BD?" I enquired.

"I don't know. Earlier some seniors came and told us to stay inside our rooms and no matter what happens no one should be seen outside. So we are all pretending to be asleep." I explained.

"I heard noises from the gym as if some guy is being beaten up." I told him.

"We heard those noises too but it is better to ignore them Himanshu. I don't want to get beaten up." He replied.

Soon I was on my bed pretending to be asleep ignoring those many screams we heard in the next hour. After that hour the screams went to sleep and so did we.

Time came very soon to leave for the competition and after bunking enough and more classes with seniors for dance practice I was finally going to be marked present for the next entire week for it was an official trip from the college. For this sole reason I had to explain to a lot of my friends to not give me proxy as I will be marked present any ways. But we were not alone who were going to dance there. A group of girls was tagging along too for their dance. And the best part about the trip was that they were fresher's, and that meant only one thing; new birds in the sanctuary. I quickly scanned through all of them and found only two potential targets, because others were either 'manchesters' up front or 'flatrons' at the back.

The train soon started moving and we were still struggling to find our seats. Fortunately Karan came and sat next to me so boredom was denied. But the more fortunate part was that one of the targets landed in the seat right in front of us. And as soon as she parked her ass both of us started deploying plots and conversations to get her attention. It was very obvious that Karan was leading as she was laughing at his jokes more. I was starting to get disheartened when Neha, as I found out her name was, got up and walked away from us. She stood next to the door and the bright sun only made her a more potential target than what she already was. The wind was blowing her long straight hair behind her face which looked prettier with every beam of sunlight falling on her skin. With her scarf almost flying away, her biggest assets, which were trying to take a peek outside her tight top, grabbed our attention. Karan and I found each other staring at that long slender artistically curved figure. I was already losing the battle and this was my only chance to take a step forward. One look at her eyes and I just knew she was waiting for one of us to make a move. I knew Karan was going for it but I could not have given up so easily.

"Hey is that your wallet on the floor under the seat?" I gestured to the floor and spoke.

"Where?" He inquired and bent down to search for it while I took a leap over him and was next to Neha in no time.

I had to make a statement right now and it had to be effective. But I also needed to know if she was single and ready to mingle.

"Seems like your breakup was so sad that you want to jump off the train?" I said with a naughty smile.

"My break up was a long time ago and it was good it happened. What about you? Did you have a sad breakup recently that this idea crossed your mind?" She replied with a question smiling at me.

Now I was falling into a trick. Was she being sarcastic or was she giving me hints and wanted to know if I was ready to mingle. I just closed my eyes and decided to go for it.

"No I haven't but I sure would like to try it."

"But don't you need to be in a relationship for a breakup?" She asked turning her entire self towards me.

"I guess so." I replied shrugging my shoulders.

Pulling her scarf down from her neck rolling it up her palm she whispered in a low tone "So what are you going to do about it?"

I grabbed the door behind her and moved myself closer to her, pushing away her chest out of my eye sight. I looked straight into her eyes and said "I'm working on it already."

She turned her face away and giggled while her cheeks got red. I turned around to see what Karan's reaction was as I knew he would have been staring at the whole scene from his seat. He was staring at us with his red angry eyes and gestured his middle finger towards me. I knew I had struck bull's eye.

We stayed in a hotel close to the venue and practiced every day in the banquet hall. In the next 5 days we had a series of events in which we all participated. On the 4th day was the boy's dance and the 5th day was the girl's dance. The results were to be declared together at the end of the program after the girl's group dance which was the last event. We were all excited about it. We had definitely made a great performance but there were more than fifteen groups participating and hence the competition standard was higher.

The results were soon declared and both of us boys and girls groups bagged the second place. It didn't feel as good as it would have if we had topped the competition but it was still a very nice feeling. This called in for a party and so we all decided to dash all night in the hotel. By the time we got to the hotel it was already past 9 pm but no one wanted to cancel the party plan. So we pushed the wardens to go to their rooms and all of us students headed to the banquet hall. We ordered a lot of food and drinks and the party started off with very loud music. People were still dancing even though this time there was no coordination at all. My phone vibrated in my pocket and the message I read made me realize that Neha wasn't around.

"Isn't d party too loud n noisy? I got bored so I left 2my rum. Mind givin me sum company?"

I stuffed my phone back into my pocket and sprinted out of the hall to her room. The corridor was empty and her room was just two doors away from the warden's room. There wasn't much light so I tip toed my way and discovered a half open door. Pushing the door open I found the room dimly lit and Neha standing on the far end of the room. I walked in without any permission even though it looked like Neha was going to change her clothes. Her saree was being pulled out by herself when I coughed to make my presence felt.

"Thank god you are here. Can you please help me with this?" she turned around and asked pointing just below her waist on the back at a clip which she apparently could not pull out herself. Even though it wasn't out of her reach, I didn't want to miss out on a chance to do such a favour to myself.

I walked in closer to her and gently lay my hand on her waist. She took a deep breath and I traced my fingers to that clip and removed it. Her saree slid off her smooth skin and landed next to our feet. She turned and took another deep breath with her eyes closed. Her lips were barely inches away from mine, both our foreheads were sweaty and her mountains were peaking at my chest.

"Did you have dinner?" I asked.

She opened her eyes wide apart and gave me a "What the fuck?" look.

"Why the fuck did you say that you retard! I cursed myself." I felt totally dumb to ask such a question at such a critical moment. She looked into my eyes, flattened the creases on her forehead, wrapped her arms around my waste and pulled me closer. Her mountains got trampled and my projection got harder. With her husky voice and her lips gently brushing against mine she said.

"I'm going to have some right now!"

I couldn't take it anymore. Fear still existed negligibly in the back of my head for it was a random hotel room we were in but how could I not use such an opportunity? I kissed her lips and hugged her tighter and stronger. I started a series of kisses down her neck which got wilder and hotter every second. She grabbed my hands and put them right where I wanted to. I grabbed them strong and squeezed them while biting her neck and all she did was struggle hard to breath. She then turned around and pushed me onto the bed. I realized that my belt was undone and so were most of my shirt buttons. I wondered when she did that and how I didn't realize it earlier. She forced me to lie down and like a cat jumped on top of me. She took a sigh and started working on her blouse. Taking out the hooks seemed difficult as there was some heavy luggage inside. With every hook undone those puppies seemed more and more eager to come out. They seemed to get bigger every time a hook popped out and so did my wood. She threw her blouse away and the puppies were barely held together by a tight black lacy push up bra making a long cleavage. I could even make out the borders of her nipples. I was starting to get really hungry now. She bent forwards holding me by my neck and placed a kiss on my lips. Then she moved towards the side and after kissing my ear she whispered "Can I start munching on my dinner now?"

With a lot of difficulty I swallowed and hummed allowing her to start her supper. I then felt my shirt pulled apart and her soft smooth lips on my chest placing kisses all around. Her hands reached my groins and my pant was being pulled down but my hands were somehow paralyzed to stop her from doing so. Not that I wanted to stop her but there was a feeling inside of me that this was not the right thing to do. This thought was completely shattered when she completely pulled out all of my clothes below the waist and put her lips and tongue to full use. It felt like heaven. I was enjoying every bit of it. Every second the feeling kept improving. Her every touch was making me grow more and more insane. I was sweating like a pig but that didn't make me stop. I pulled myself up to a sitting position and held her by her hair helping her take it deeper. She looked at me with those wild hungry eyes and I completely lost myself.

"It's time for me to munch on you now." I said while struggling for breath.

"Nope, you are my senior. Let me do the job today." She said winking at me filling her mouth again. Soon her mountains were showered with the rain and the job was well done.

The gang was still busy with the party when I got back to my room. Things between me and Neha went too fast and I didn't even have a chance to realize what potential the relation had. Wait; there wasn't even a relationship yet. I hadn't asked her out yet and we had done so much already. This definitely meant that there will not be a potential in this relationship, if at all it becomes one. But was this right? I was never in a just for benefit kind of a relationship yet even though my last experience with Urvashi did guide me towards this. Could I go on with this? I decided to not let this bother me for the time being and slept off.

There we were standing in front of the principal's office all ready to express our happiness on winning the dance competition. Being the leader of the group I was standing up front with the trophy in my hand. The secretary came out and called me in. I walked in and found the entire DISCO waiting there for us. I was a little confused for I didn't know why all of them would be there, to congratulate us? That could not have been the reason. I smelt something fishy.

As soon as I acquired a position from where I could see all of them familiar faces but one, all the 6 members of the DISCO fired questions upon me.

"Where were you last Friday?" The Principal shot the first question.

With a confused state and expression I confessed my presence in the mess hall along with the rest of the group for dance practice.

"Till what time did you practice?" He shot another one.

"Till around 10 pm sir." I replied.

"And what did you do after that?" The third question came from Dr. C.G. Nayar.

"I went to my room to sleep." I replied.

"Did you hear anything or see any one with awkward behaviour?" The Principal asked again.

"No sir not that I can remember." I confessed.

"He telling lie. I'm told you he involved in whole thing. He telling lie."

Now there was the retard that I could not identify from the DISCO members. She was old, in her mid-40s, dressed in entire white attire. She definitely looked irritated and more annoying probably because she wasn't satisfied enough. And clearly she knew English very well.

"I'm not lying. I don't know what you are talking about. I only came here to let you know that we got the second place in the inter college dance competition. That is all. Can I leave now?" I asked sternly.

The bitch in the white saree started blabbering again while I was leaving the room. All my seniors were waiting outside for their turn to be called in. I knew it was related to what had happened that night. So I took Karan to one side and inquired about it.

"I don't know what happened Himanshu, don't ask me." Karan tried to divert the topic.

"Dude you were there that day. And you were the one who asked me to stay inside my room if I didn't want to get in trouble. You obviously knew what was happening." I trapped him.

"Himanshu let's not get into this please." He continued avoiding the topic.

"Either you are going to tell me or else I'm going to say something to the bitch in white saree." I threatened him.

"Who? RC? No no no, don't you even think of doing that in your wildest dreams. Fine I'll tell you but you can't tell anyone about this ok. That night we beat up Akarsh Gupta." He confessed.

"What the fuck? Why?" I was shocked.

"He was the spy from our batch. He used to tell about who all have mobile phones, i-pods, which girl is dating which guy, who all bunk classes and go to the city and everything else, even about drinking and porn stuff. We tried to tell him not to do that but he didn't listen to us and continued with his ass licking so we decided to teach him a lesson." He elaborated.

"Does he know it was you guys?" I enquired.

"No we put a bed sheet around his head while he was walking back from the bathroom. He did not see anyone. We dragged him down to the gym. We needed that loud music so that no one hears him scream while we dragged him to the gym. After that we stopped the dance practice remember? Then we went in by turns and whacked his good for nothing ass with rubber pipes and tennis rackets. One of our seniors got too excited and hit him too hard and broke his arm. Then he fell unconscious and we had to take him to the casualty. We were all scared to death but fortunately before it became a big issue we left for the dance competition. It was very dark in there and his face was covered so he could not identify anyone of us but these bastards are calling everyone in individually and interrogating. Even if a single person breaks we are all dead. What are we going to do?" He narrated the entire story.

"You guys are crazy you know that right?" I said.

"It's not funny Himanshu; our careers may just get fucked." Karan was freaking out.

"Who all took him to the casualty that night?" I asked.

"I don't know man, how does that even matter?" He was losing his mind.

"I'm trying to help you retard!" For a second I thought I went too far but then it was such an intense situation he didn't even realize I called him a retard.

"Sasi, Sijith, Ankit and Kiran."

"Just go in and tell them that you saw Akarsh ragging someone near the stairs and he was getting physical with the junior. And you tried to save the junior and he got hurt. Then you took him to the casualty." I tried to make up a story to help them.

"What? How do we explain his broken arm? And why would we beat him up to save a junior?" He questioned me.

"Fine give me a second. Do one thing, tell them that Akarsh Gupta was ragging one of the juniors you don't know who, and then he got physical and to escape him the junior probably pushed him down the stairs during which he broke his arm and fell unconscious. And by the time you ran up to see who pushed him, there was no one there." I modified the story.

"Yes that will explain his broken arm too, and to help him we took him to the casualty." His light bulb got lit.

He called all the guys waiting there and told them the plot. But there was one problem. Ankit had already gone in and none of us knew how much he would have confessed.

"Fuck. We are all going to be chucked out of college in no time." Sasi expressed his concern.

We were all eagerly waiting for Ankit to come out and to find out if there was still any way possible to escape the accusation.

While we were all sweating and struggling to think of any other ideas Ankit walked out of the principal's office.

"Dude what did you tell them?" Karan asked Ankit.

"I told them nothing! Wasn't that the plan?" He replied.

"Like nothing at all?" Karan insisted.

"Nope." Ankit replied.

"Fuck, now we are even more fucked. Now if we tell this story they will ask Ankit why he didn't confess earlier." Mohammad was really scared.

"Let's just say he was really scared to confess. Wait does anyone know that Ankit was with us when we took Akarsh to the casualty? Ankit did you tell them that you were there?" Karan enquired.

"No dude, I told them that I was in my room studying with music I couldn't even have heard if anything happened just outside my room." Ankit explained.

"Perfect. Himanshu you go on now, if they see you around here for longer they'll suspect you again. Rest of you guys listen. We are going to stick to the plan with the only difference being that Ankit was not involved in all of this. It was just the three of you who took him to the casualty alright?" Karan had turned back to his gang.

While I was walking away I heard the secretary calling Karan and winking at me he walked into the interrogation room. After that day neither did we ever discuss what happened that night with Akarsh Gupta and nor did we discuss the happenings of inside that room with the DISCO. Later that week Akarsh Gupta was transferred to Trivandrum medical college for his own safety.

Chapter Fourteen

"HER DARKNESS OF SEDUCTION"

It had been few months into our second year and our surgery posting was already over. We were now going to enter the medicine department and we were more worried as the professors in the medicine department were known to be more terrifying than the brigadier.

I sat up till late night with BD to study case taking in Malayalam so that I wouldn't make a fool out of myself the next day. So in a half drowsy state I reached the medicine department where we discovered our division into different units. I was the first person in the 2nd unit whose chief was Dr, Bhaskar. I almost shat in my pants when I found this out as I had heard enough and more from my seniors about this devil. And being the 1st person in the unit it was most likely that it would be my fucking day today to do the case presentation. We met the department secretary to know the where about of Dr. Bhaskar. He had given the details of the case to be taken to the secretary and after collecting them we headed to the general wards. Some of my unit mates took it very lightly and decided to go on a tea break even before the devil had showed up. But me and Roshan were shit scared and decided to stay with the patient and take his history for starters.

We had just started taking the history of the patient and hadn't even completed the bio-data when an old man walked in close, and stood on the other side of the bed. He was wearing thick framed spectacles and had very shabby hair. He hadn't shaved in days together and was wearing a white, which had now turned to a shade of brown, shirt with a pair of black pants which were almost worn out at the edges. His sole was separated from the floor by a very thin layer of his worn out chappals. His feet were rough and cracked at many areas. His hands and arms had scales and needed some moisturizing lotion desperately. We assumed he was one of the patient's relatives. We ignored his presence and continued with the case taking. Roshan continued reading the book and telling me the questions which I had to ask. As I was better than him in speaking Malayalam I was asking the questions to the patient even though the patient's response were equally not understood by either of us. After few minutes we somehow managed to take a very brief history with a lot of difficulty.

"I think this much is enough Himanshu." Roshan suggested.

"But we haven't even asked him any negative history yet." I replied.

"That's ok man, it is our first day. This Bhaskar guy cannot be rude with us. How can he expect us to know so much on the first day?"

At this point the old man gave us a very angry stare and I knew something was wrong. We had never seen Dr Bhaskar before and so the possibility of him being Dr Bhaskar popped in my head. Unfortunately my suspicion was correct and he turned out to be that devil.

"What do you think you idiots are doing? Is this how you take a case?" He grabbed Roshan's text book and threw it in the air away from us.

"How can you take a case while reading from your book? And to you young man, I'm not going to be rude, I'm going to be very rude with you." He said staring at Roshan.

Roshan's legs were now shivering and I was so afraid I couldn't even swallow.

"And where is the rest of your batch. I was told that there will be a total of 12 students. Where are the other ten idiots?"

"I don't know sir." Roshan did the mistake of answering back his question.

"You don't know? How can you not know? You don't know how to take history of a patient, you don't know how to examine a patient, and you don't even know how to respect your professors. What do you know?" He was now screaming at us.

By this time Suraj and the rest of the idiots came and realised it was not the best time to join the class. They were about to turn around and leave when Dr. Bhaskar, for some reason, turned around and caught them red handed.

"Hello? Where do you think all of you are you going? Is this the time to come for the class? Where were all of you till now? Why didn't you report in time? Only these two idiots were here taking a case and they don't even know how to do that. This is a pathetic batch. Why am I given the worst students always?" He continued yelling at us while Suraj and the rest of them came closer and stood by our sides.

"What is your name?" He asked looking towards me.

I stepped forward to answer his question.

"I'm not asking you to step out and stand separately. You are not some politician's son that I should respect you so much. I just asked your name. Don't you have enough brains to answer that? Or did you forget your name also?"

"My name is Himanshu, sir." I replied.

"Ok Himanshu, present the case." He ordered.

I was really scared and my pulse was shooting up. I opened up my notebook in which I had written the details of the case and was getting ready to present.

"Hello? Are you going to stand in the crowd and present? Don't you have the common sense that if you are presenting you should step aside separately and present. Now move to one side and present." He humiliated me.

I took two steps away from the crowd and opened up my book and was hoping the humiliation would stop but there was more coming my way. As soon as I opened my note book Dr Bhaskar snatched it away from me and threw it in the air the same way he threw Roshan's textbook.

"You are not going to have a notebook in your exam to look and present. Now present the case!" He commanded.

"The patient's name is Bhaskar. He is 60 years old and a farmer by ocupa . . . ."

"Is that how you start your case? This is ridiculous. You don't even know the basics of a case presentation." He interrupted me.

After taking a very short pause he started again.

"What does the name of a patient tell you?"

We all kept quiet.

"I'm asking you Himanshu; tell me what does the name of a patient tell you?" He asked me specifically this time.

"I don't know sir." I was even scared to open my mouth but somehow managed to utter those words.

"It tells you nothing. Name of the patient is not important at all in a case presentation. Most of the textbooks even suggest that you keep the patient anonymous. Now tell me what do you ask the patient next?" He asked me again.

"The age and gender sir." I replied.

"Age is fine but how are you going to ask about the gender of the patient? Are you going to ask if he is male or female?" He was being sarcastic.

Rahul who was one of the ten idiots, smirked at this question but unfortunately Dr. Bhaskar's eyes caught him.

"Hey you, the short one with specs, get out of my class! Right now!" He screamed really loud.

Rahul was so scared of his gestures that he ran away as fast as he could.

"All of you are idiots. You don't even know how to take a case. At home my wife and children keep bothering me. And here all of you do that. Do you have any idea how it feels to have a wife who always keeps complaining because I'm not giving her enough time. I'm working in the hospital not cheating on her. And when I come here to have some peace of mind you retards make me lose my temper again. Now tell me Himanshu, don't you have a book which you could have read and come prepared to take the case?"

"I could have sir." It started to seem like he was trying to control his temper.

"Then why didn't you study and come you idiot? You think I'm a fool to come here and waste so much of time with all of you trying to break my head and teach you something. Get one thing in your head all of you. I'm not like the other teachers here. I'm not going to spoon feed you anything. If you want to learn something, do it yourself, I can only guide you. Now get lost all of you. And if you are not prepared tomorrow then don't even bother coming." He blasted us and walked away.

My hunger died with the way Dr Bhaskar treated us. So I skipped lunch and decided to go for the afternoon classes straight away. I and Roshan entered the boy's elevator from the ground floor and pressed the 10th floor button. The elevator stopped on the 1st floor and a bunch of girls entered in. Apparently the girl's elevator wasn't working so they hijacked ours. I recognized a familiar face moving towards me from the crowd and in no time Neha was standing right next to me. I felt an air of naughtiness the second her hands touched mine. She slowly moved her hand backward and pinched my bum. Now the naughtiness had entirely turned into a level of discomfort. We were in an elevator filled with girls and even though no one could see her hands I still felt uncomfortable. When the elevator reached the 10th floor everyone started getting out and on her way out she whispered to me "When do I get my sweet dish again?"

All of a sudden the devil face of Dr. Bhaskar vanished from my thoughts replaced by that night. But I wasn't in a mood to fantasize right now. I was too tired to do so. Taking a seat next to my roommate in the class I drowned in my thoughts again.

"Himanshu I forgot my book in the library, remind me to take it before we go for our practical after this class ok." BD said to me as the pathology professor walked in to the class. Soon the pathology class started and my mind started wandering like always.

"Himanshu you are still not over Urvashi, you need to move on. Go on and date Neha. She is hot, loves having sex and doesn't even complain! What is wrong with you?" My mind was talking to me. When I agreed it continued "Now that you are going to date Neha, you need to find a way to meet her often because you don't want to miss out on all the good stuff she has to offer."

"Himanshu, get up madam is calling you." BD said trying to wake me up.

"What?" I asked.

"Dude get up!" He exclaimed.

I was so lost in my thoughts that I had no idea what was going on in the class. BD told me that the professor was calling me so I stood up without any questions.

"Very good, we have a volunteer!" The teacher jumped in joy.

I gave an angry confused stare to BD realizing he had got me in to something fishy.

"What is your name?" The teacher asked.

"Himanshu." I replied.

"So you are going to make a presentation on the topic opportunistic infections next week. I'm so glad we have a volunteer. I didn't expect it though. I'm impressed. Now let us take your attendance." She continued.

Taking my seat I expressed my gratitude to BD with my middle finger. Once the attendance was taken we took the stairs down to the library as he had to take his record. I was prohibited in to the library by myself so I waited outside for him. While I was waiting a soothing voice dragged my mind away from the day's happenings.

"Hey Himanshu, remember me? I'm Roshika!"

Lost in my thoughts thinking if I've ever met her before, I shook her hands and enquired "And how do you know me?"

"Come on we have all heard enough and more about you. By the way, I have to tell you, your dance in the arts festival was just too good. I mean we were all on our feet cheering for you." She explained.

"Really?" Now she was making it very obvious that she was coming on to me. But who was she? I mean I hadn't even heard of her, and how come I never noticed this beautiful piece of art before.

"Trust me Himanshu, seniors standing up and cheering for you, that is something!" She spoke again.

"Yup that is!" I smirked, smiling at my bad luck that I found a hottie hitting on me who was a senior. So there was no scope what so ever.

"So what else is going on with you?" She asked.

"Nothing really. I have microbiology practicals at . . . oh my God its 2 already" glancing at my watch I reacted.

"Very sorry chechi but I have to go now." I continued.

"Hey Himanshu, you can call me Roshika. No more chechi ok." She said winking at me.

"Alright! See you later." I said in a confused voice and ran up the stairs leaving behind Roshan and the other jerks as I didn't want to get screwed again.

Reaching class I realized my entire batch was inside on their seats. Fortunately Roshan had saved a seat for me next to him. I asked for permission to enter the room and quickly jumped in to that seat.

"Open your records and start copying the matter on these slides with the same format on to the first page" The 5 feet 5 inches tall professor with a 5 cm thick moustache spoke.

"How the fuck did you guys reach here before me?" I asked Roshan.

"You were busy talking to that bitch so we thought we shouldn't disturb you." He explained.

"You should have called me dude. And why is she a bitch?" I asked.

"See, she is hot and sexy, everyone wants to fuck her but can't. So she is a bitch!" He reasoned.

"What?" I was confused with that reason.

"Just go with it ok." He responded.

"Ok fine." I replied.

"You on the 3rd row, get up!" The teacher screamed.

And all of us in perfect coordination turned around to see who that unlucky person was.

"Why are you looking at your back? Look forwards at me." He screamed again.

And again with the same coordination everyone turned their heads front.

"Now you, the boy sitting on the third row get up." He clarified.

This time when we turned around we realized that the third row was full of girls. We were all confused when he jumped down the deck and walked towards us.

After a few short swift steps, the migid stood right in front of me, staring at me with his red eyes.

"You think you are very smart? I've been asking you to stand up so many times and you are not listening to me?" He screamed at me.

"Sir but you said the third row?" I tried to defend myself.

"So you don't even have the simple common sense to know that you are sitting on the third row?" He challenged my common sense now.

"Sir this is the 1st row, and I'm sitting on the third column." I replied boldly.

Now the professor was taken aback. He probably realized his "simple common sense" was stupid but it was obvious that he wasn't going to accept it. So even before he could ask me I started packing my bag.

"You think you are very much smart? You think you know more than me? Boy I have been teaching for 10 years now and you think you can come in my class and not listen to . . . . wait where are you going?" He questioned me.

"Sir I thought you would yell at me and eventually ask me to get out so I was saving your energy and going out myself." I replied.

"Now you are acting too smart. Get back here and sit on your seat." He screamed again.

So I turned back around and sat on my seat.

"Your professor is yelling at you and you are sitting down in front of him?" He continued screaming.

"Sir but you asked me to sit down?" I tried to question him.

"So shameless boy you are. Get out of my class right now!" Pointing at the door he exclaimed.

What was his problem? When I was going out he called me in and then he chucks me out. May be professors like yelling on students and asking them to get out. Probably when I was going out myself his ego was hurt as I didn't give him a chance to yell at me. But I never really understood why I was caught in the first place.

Once I got out of the classroom I realized I left my bag inside but I couldn't have gone back in. So I went and sat on the back stairs and almost dozed off to sleep when that same soothing voice woke me up.

"I thought you had practical class now, then why are you sitting here?" Roshika asked me.

"I was kicked out of class, but my bag and books are still inside. So I am waiting for that donkey to finish and leave the class room so that I can take my books and go back to the hostel." I explained.

"Awwww that's so sad" saying that she pulled my cheeks.

"Anyways don't you have class now?" I asked.

"Hmmm, actually I'm late myself. Do you mind if I sit here with you for some time?" She asked.

"No not at all. Have a seat." I moved aside.

"So what else is going on with you? Made a girlfriend yet?" She enquired placing herself on the same stair, close to me.

Considering she was coming on to me a lot in the recent meeting near the library, this kind of behaviour did not surprise me even a little and I let her brush her body against my arm.

"No not yet." I wasn't sure if I should have told her about Neha because if you actually think about it neither of us asked either of us out. So basically we weren't really dating. At least that way I justified myself for if I had told her that I had a girlfriend that would take off that slight amount of attention that I was getting from her. More over even if I was dating Neha, it wouldn't have been a big crime to bite two apples together as I wasn't up for anything serious considering I had been hurt enough and more already with Urvashi.

Suddenly she got up and pulled my hand.

"Himanshu lets go." She whispered.

"Go where?" I asked.

"Someone is coming down. Hurry up." She whispered again.

The thought of getting caught with a girl and ending up in another suspension crossed my mind and before I could think of anything else my legs stood up in reflex and followed hers into the bathroom close by. There were 6 different cubicles and we were standing near the wash basins.

"Come on come inside in here." She said opening the door of the last cubicle.

"In there?" I asked surprisingly.

"You don't want to get caught do you?" She asked.

I shut my mouth up and with my head down walked into the cubicle and she locked the door behind. There was pin drop silence and this desperation of doing something to her developed inside my mind. I mean who wouldn't think that way, almost dark, empty bathroom, no one around and the girl is the one who brought you into all this. Why wouldn't anyone's mind slip? But still she was my senior and if I mess up anything that would mean that I would lose all the support that I have from my seniors. So instead of making a move myself, I waited for her.

After few more seconds she finally took a deep breath and moved closer to me. She put her arms on my shoulders and pushed herself up on her toes to bring her face very close to mine. I was surely expecting a kiss on my lips or at least on my cheeks. Instead she strafed to the side till her lips gently touched my ears. Her body was almost falling into mine. I could feel her clothes touching mine but there wasn't any body contact yet. Our hips were very close to each other but yet not one.

"Isn't it boring in here? You want to do something?" She whispered.

Placing my hands on her hips I asked "Something like what?"

"Oh my God, no Himanshu I didn't mean to do something like that. I meant like talk or something because we still have to wait for some more time before we can go." She replied with hesitation.

"Oh ok. So what do you want to talk about?" With a slightly disappointed face I whispered back.

"Wait you actually thought I was making a move on you?" She whispered into my ears.

"Oh no, obviously not. I mean why would you do that?" I asked back.

"Why can't I?" She whispered that question into my ears, moved her face back while the rest of her body was sinking into mine. She gave me a naughty look and all the positions possible in that small cubicle flashed in my head.

Her hands from my shoulders slowly went across my neck and suddenly she was hugging on to me really tight. I also realized that my hands had slipped down inside her pants on to her ass and she didn't seem to mind it either. I made a good grip with my hands and pulled her up. She swung her legs around me and crossed them behind my waist. The next thing I know was that her clothes were off, my pants were pulled down and I was inside her already. We were vigorously smooching and I gave her all the reasons to moan and scream. While I was sweating and thrusting harder I heard footsteps entering the bathroom. I stopped moving but held on to her really tight and close. The footsteps soon entered the cubicle next to ours and I almost stopped breathing. This was when Roshika tightened her legs around my waist and started dancing her hips back and forth. It was a good move but the fear of someone over hearing us made me lose my wood in the jungle. I gently pulled myself from her and placed her down on her feet. While I was trying to pull my pants up without making any noise, she came close and whispered "you are not going anywhere till I'm done with you. Now stand still and let go of your pants."

She was my senior and I had to listen to her. More over the footsteps had vacated the bathroom and we had time for more action. She sat down on the seat and grabbed my ass pulling me closer. Soon she started working on me and now only my lips were free to moan. I grabbed her hair and helped her go faster when suddenly the light went off. This scared me a little and the thought of getting caught crossed my mind.

"Don't think that the darkness is going to stop me." She whispered.

And in the darkness of her seduction I didn't even realize when and where I climaxed.

I was really scared stepping out of that bathroom once Roshika had left. I still pushed myself out of there and moved to the classroom and found out that the class was over and everyone was gone including my bag. So I made my walk to the hostel. When I entered the corridor of my wing, I heard a lot of murmur coming from the room across mine. I took a peek to see which crowd was sitting there and unfortunately they all saw me too.

"Dude where were you, I didn't find you so I brought back your bag here. I kept it in our room." BD said to me.

"Oye wait, first tell me what was going on in front of the library today?" Roshan asked me.

"What are you talking about?" I asked in return.

"Himanshu, even I saw you with that bitch, what was going on?" Raunak questioned me.

"Bitch? Oh yeah I remember the reason. I was just talking to her, what is the big deal in that?" I replied.

"No big deal man. Tomorrow you will come and say that you had sex with her but it won't be a big deal at all for you." Suman expressed his thought.

"Nothing like that bro, she came to me and we just had a conversation." I explained.

"So tell me, how do her boobs look up close?" Roshan asked with a lot of expectations for a good description.

"Excuse me? I did not have a look at them." Even though they were the best set I had ever seen so far I could not have made a comment on it.

"I can't believe you. She was standing right in front of you and you didn't look?" Roshan asked with a disappointed face.

"No I didn't." I replied.

"Come on Himanshu tell us already." Suman requested.

"I am going to go back to my room now!" I declared.

"Dude wait we are not done." Raunak tried to stop me.

I ignored their requests for me to stay back in that room and got back into mine and collapsed on my bed. The thought cloud started raining again and got me into some serious thinking. I was glad Roshika didn't have my number so she would not call me. Getting into a serious relation thing with her would cause more damage than good especially if she finds out about Neha. More over Neha was much better than her in the aspects I was lately more interested in. So I picked up my phone and called Neha. While I was talking to her I got a message which read—"Hey im sorry v cud nt tok aftr wht hapnd 2day, bt im sure I dont need 2 tel u tht u shudnt mention it 2 any1 about wht hapnd on 6ᵗʰ floor 2day. Im also sure I'l accidentally meet u thr sumtym soon agn n mayb v cn plan tht accident ☺"

Even though the number wasn't from my contact list it was obvious that it was Roshika. But I had made my mind not to get involved with a senior like this again even if it was the same one. So instead of responding to Roshika's message I continued talking and planned the accident with Neha.

Chapter Fifteen

"IT'S BEEN 4EVR HASN'T IT?"

It had been weeks since I discovered the new hot spot, thanks to Roshika, and I had been visiting the same several times, sometime twice a day, but not with her. I started bunking classes more often in the afternoon to find pleasure instead of knowledge. But now it had started to get obvious to other people. I and Neha were seen on several occasions together at different locations, canteen, juice stall, library steps etc. So after many days of serious exercise in the 6th floor bathroom I decided to actually stay back and talk to Neha for some time and maybe end it. So there I was pulling my pants back up while she was busy with her hooks.

"Hey, I had something to talk to you." I whispered to Neha.

"Oh yeah tell me." She whispered back.

"Not now, maybe once you are dressed." This was when I realized for the first time that you always help the other person undress but never help them dress up.

"Ok. How about we go to the juice stall after this?" She suggested.

"Yeah that will work." I agreed.

"I will quickly dress up and meet you there. Here is my bag and my phone. You go ahead and wait for me there unless you want to stare at me dressing myself." She asked.

"I think I'll wait for you there." I replied.

"Ok see you there in 10 ok." She whispered again.

I hummed and with utmost precautions stepped out of the bathroom and left for the juice stall. It was a Saturday afternoon and the girls had permission to go home. Even Neha was going to visit her local guardian this weekend so I thought of telling her before she leaves. While I was waiting for her in the juice stall thinking of ways I could end it her phone buzzed with a text. I ignored it the first time but I could not control my curiosity after her phone buzzed the 4th time.

I unlocked her phone to open the new message section which showed 4 new texts from Varun.

I was shocked when I read the contents.

"Hey r u sure u r comin home 2nyt? U sure ur aunt wont suspect?"

"1 more thing, remembr v finished d condoms lst week u came here. So dont 4gt 2 gt a pack on ur way. Actually gt 2 im sure its goin 2b a long weekend ☺"

"Hello u thr??"

"Y r u nt respondin baby?"

For a second I was breathless reading them. But then it struck me as the perfect reason and actually a genuine one to break it up with her. That day I broke up with a girl for the first time. And thankfully it was me dumping her. She gave a lot of lame excuses and tried to clarify but it was very obvious from those messages about what exactly she was up to.

"No Neha. I don't want to listen any more. This is it. I can't believe you did this to me. How could you?"

"But Himanshu please listen to . . ."

"Neha just shut up ok. This is enough to handle already. I don't want to listen to your crap any more. You are going away this weekend and when you get back we are going to be nothing but senior and junior. Get that thing in your head." I almost yelled at her getting up from my chair.

After taking few steps away from her I stopped and turned around.

"And yeah, don't forget to buy TWO packs of condoms for your Varun, seems like you both are going to have a long weekend." And I walked out on her while she was still sitting there with her face down. This time the groups of other students sitting on the close by tables heard me but I didn't care at all and I left cursing her in my head.

I was frustrated and tired and all I wanted was to get away from Neha as far away as possible. After reaching my room the only thing I remember was a glimpse of my bed and then BD poking me with my badminton racket the next morning. He used to use the racket as a protective shield in case I turn violent after waking up.

"Himanshu get up, we have a meeting now." BD told me.

"What meeting?" I asked.

"Arts festival is coming up in a month and we have to start practicing man." He replied.

"Where is it?" I asked again.

"In the mess hall!" He responded.

"When is it?" I asked again.

"Right now!!" He almost screamed.

"Fine I'll be there in some time, you go ahead." I replied calmly.

BD left the room and I got up picking up my phone. There were many more texts from Neha which I deleted without even reading it. There was one more message that read "hey u! hows it going? Its been 4evr hasn't it? yup its been 4evr! ;)"

As it was from an unknown number I ignored it. I quickly freshened up and rushed to the mess hall to join the meeting in progress.

"Himanshu, thank God you are here. You are in charge of the dance group. Pick on the people and the songs and start the practice soon. And don't worry about the props and costumes; we'll help you with all that later ok." Our class rep told me.

"Is that it?" BD who was sitting close by took a glance at me and I flipped him off for making me get up and come all this way for something I knew already.

I took a lazy walk back to my room and I checked my phone. I read a text and made a call. While I was on the call my phone buzzed again. It had a text from Roshika.

"Meet me at d lib at 12. Its imp"

I looked at my watch and it was 11.30 already. It was a Sunday so the 6th floor would be closed and no matter what I wasn't going to get involved with her in any sort of activity. So I decided to go.

"Hey" I wished Roshika from a distance while she was waiting for me near the library steps.

"Come here." She almost ordered me.

"What happened?" I asked.

"Tell me frankly, how many people did you talk to about us meeting up on the 6th floor?" She asked with anger.

"No one!" I answered.

"Are you sure?" She asked for confirmation.

"Yes 100 percent." I replied.

"And did you go there with someone else?" She questioned me further.

I wasn't sure of what to reply to that and so I started looking here and there.

"Himanshu tell me." She ordered.

"Why are you asking me such questions Roshika?" I asked.

"Did you go there with Neha or not?" She questioned.

"What? Who told you that?" I was shocked.

"She did herself. Now tell me if you mentioned me to any one?" She continued questioning.

"No Roshika I didn't I swear. But what did Neha tell you?" I asked her politely.

"Not just me. She is telling the entire world how you used her in there. How you used to go there so often and have sex with her." She responded.

"What?" I was shocked yet again.

"She is screwing up big time Himanshu." Roshika explained.

"But why would she do that? That's also going to screw up her reputation right?" I tried to reason.

"I don't know Himanshu. But you better take care of this mess. I just wanted to tell you that. Take care."

She walked away leaving me confused and angry. Only a day had passed since I had dumped her and she had started showing me her true colours already. I took out my phone to call Neha but then I realized that she probably wouldn't take my call as she was with someone else now. So I decided to let it go and let the matter dissolve itself with time.

Over the next few days I got many stares from almost every girl that crossed me. Some of them were angry stares, some full of shame and most of them murmured something the second they saw me. Things had gone way beyond limits and I had to do something about it. So I decided to confront Neha. I went straight to the medicine department where she was posted and asked her to come out of the demonstration hall. I did get some similar stares from her batch mates but I cared less.

"Yes Himanshu?" She asked with a lot of attitude.

"What the fuck is wrong with you Neha? Why are you talking shit about me to people?" I asked angrily.

"Why do you care what I talk to people? You walked out on me in the juice stall remember?" She replied.

"Does that mean that you will go and tell people about our personal stuff?" I was furious.

She kept quiet.

"Tell me Neha what are you getting out of this?" I asked calming myself down.

"I freaked out ok. That day you yelled at me and left me in tears. And my friends who were sitting next to our table heard you screaming. They came

157

and asked me what went wrong and I had to tell them something right?" She confessed.

"So what did you tell them?" I asked.

"I told them that you dumped me." She replied.

"And I dumped you because?" I asked again.

She kept quiet again.

"Tell me Neha what did you tell them?" I insisted.

"I told them that we used to have sex a lot and when I refused for such kind of a relationship you dumped me." She explained.

"What the fuck? Was that the reason?" I asked getting angry again.

"No but I didn't know what else to tell them." She had almost started crying.

"So you screwed me over. What is wrong with you Neha? Do you know how bad it's going to be for you? And couldn't you think of any other reason? Why did you have to screw me over like this?" I asked.

"I'm sorry Himanshu I just didn't know what else to tell them." Tears were rolling down her cheeks now.

"This is the dumbest thing you could have done Neha. You made up this mess and you are going to clean it up. Don't ask me how because I don't know but you have to." I said angrily.

"I'm really sorry Himanshu. I promise I'll make it up to you somehow." She replied.

"Be sorry to yourself Neha." And I walked away.

For several days I kept getting those dirty stares but it bothered me less now. Arts festival was in a few days and I was focusing more on the dance practice as I had to do another solo part in the middle. The dance practices went very late in the nights and even early mornings on weekends but that didn't make us stop practicing.

Soon the arts festival arrived and we were paid off for our hard work. The crowd was still on their feet screaming their throats out when we got off the stage. I got a lot of pats on my back and congratulations as I made my walk through the crowd out of the auditorium. I was thirsty and desperately needed some water, so I walked to the water cooler. While I was gulping down water a hand touched my shoulder. I turned around to find Neha standing there with a smile. I was confused but I had to ask what was wrong and why she was smiling so much.

"Himanshu, remember I told you that I will make it up to you somehow?" She asked.

"Yeah so?" I was still angry.

"Come with me." She requested.

I followed her to the entrance of the auditorium where a pretty girl was standing waiting for her.

"Where did you go Neha?" The pretty girl asked Neha.

"Hey this is Himanshu." Neha introduced me.

"Oh hi Himanshu!" She said pushing her hand forward.

"Ummm hi?" Shaking her hands I replied.

"This is Reena by the way, she has just joined. She was my junior in school." Neha elaborated.

"Ohh ok." I reacted.

"I'm going to leave you two here ok, I have to go do something." And Neha left.

"By the way your dance was awesome." Reena expressed her thoughts.

"Thanks." I replied.

"Have you learned it somewhere or your feet just dance to the music?" She asked.

"I never really learned dancing, just one of those things I'm good at I guess. Anyways they are going to announce the results now so maybe I'll catch up with you later some time?" I tried to strafe away.

"Sure. Oh and I'm sure your group is going to win." With a smile she declared.

And so we did. This time we ruled over the entire festival. Dance, songs, instruments, you name an event and we had a winner from our batch in that. And because we won the overall championship our batch decided to stay back and party on the last day. We played loud music and danced a lot. After sometime I got really tired and sat down in one corner while the rest of the crowd continued to move in a way they called dancing. After making sure that no one from the administration was around I took out my phone to check if I had any calls. I had a text message.

"Hey this is Reena, sorry cudnt ask u 4 ur no so hd 2 ask Neha, hope u dnt mind"

"Na thts fine. Ryt nw im stil in d auditorium so mayb I'l give u a col a lil latr? I replied.

"Sure, bt dnt make me wait 4 too long :p"

And so my late night calls and monthly phone bills started to increase again. Soon after the arts festival was our 2ⁿᵈ year final exams. Even though I and Reena used to speak a lot over the phone, she used to push me a lot to study. So it wasn't really a hindrance for my exams.

Chapter Sixteen

"EAR NOSE AND WHAT?"

The exams came in and flew by. Preparation was less, time on the phone was more and answers on the papers were less, very less. Even then I somehow managed to pass. Reena was a constant help that made me keep going the entire month. Actually if she wasn't there I would have kept going anyways but her presence had made me lose interest in books again. Even though we were just friends it was fun talking to her as our conversations mostly led in a direction where we would end up being more than friends. Those many times we met were all non-physical and I was glad I wasn't in a relationship which was only just about sex. Well that was definitely a necessity but I wasn't looking forward to just that. The way I was hurt after Urvashi and what Neha did, kept me on my toes but I felt a little different about Reena. I knew either something really great was going to happen between the both of us or something very terrible. For now it looked like it was going well but I wasn't so sure.

The entire three weeks that I spent at home waiting for my results, I was in touch with Reena. Calls, texts, mails and chats and still no signs of anything that would make things go wrong. Sometimes we did end up into something naughty but either her friends would come into the room or my parents would break the air. Moreover I wasn't ready to get into something like that. So by the time I got back to college I was really looking forward to meet her and see where things would go. My new posting was in the department of ENT and because the HOD was also the principal, things were really strict here. I barely used to get time to talk to my friends properly, so forget me meeting Reena. It was just a month that we were into our new year and we were thrown upon a test. Our ENT posting was about to end in another week and so they decided to take an end posting exam to figure out how well they have taught us. It was a batch of 20 people and each student was supposed to take a case and present it to one of the two senior most professors of the department which included the principal as well.

We were given 30 minutes to take the respective cases and then we were made to wait in a class room and two students were called in at a time for the viva. The first two went in and the rest of us flipped through the pages of our brand new ENT book quickly. In less than 10 minutes the first two came out and the 3rd and 4th person were called in. The principal was taking odd numbers, my number was the sixth one from the top and so I was sure not to get the principal. But unfortunately somehow when the 5th person and I walked into the room, some confusion happened and I ended up sitting in front of the principal. I was shit scared to even open my mouth.

"Do I have to plead you to start your case presentation?" The Principal said to me.

"No sir, I'm presenting a case of a 32 year old male patient who came with complaints of discharge from the right ear . . ." I started my case presentation.

Two case presentations were going on side by side with the two professors. It was very distracting as we had both taken similar cases and while we were presenting the professors kept themselves busy going through our case sheets. I was trying to focus on my friend's presentation to check if I'm missing out a point when the principal started firing me with questions in the middle of my case presentation. I didn't know the answers to most of his questions and even though I kept my mouth shut the silence was filled with angry words from the principal which accused me of not reading and wasting time in the hostel all the time. While he was busy scolding me I was paying attention to the question answer series going on the next table, and I was surprised to see how it could be so entirely different.

"So tell me, what have you observed in the last whole month of your posting here?" The lady professor asked Roshan.

"Cleaning ears and nose!" Roshan replied.

"Oh my god, now he is going to get some from the professor." I thought in my head.

But fortunately for him the old female professor burst out in laughter and moved on to the next question.

"You at least know what department you are posted in right?" She asked.

"Yes mam, ENT!" Roshan said with a smile.

"Ok but what is it actually called?" She asked again.

"It's called Otorhinolaryngology you idiot, tell her that!" I screamed in my head.

He kept quiet.

"At least tell me the full form of ENT and I'll let you go." She said with smirk.

"Ear, nose and . . ." and then he paused for a second and looked at me.

I opened my mouth and pointed inside.

He smile at me, turned to the professor and said "Tongue."

And I slapped my palm on my forehead.

"Yes that is all that you will do if you don't study. Now leave the room and next time you come here you better have answers." The Principal scolded me.

"Yes sir!" And I got up to leave with Roshan.

The second we stepped out of that room I slapped Roshan on the back of his head and said "Ear nose and TONGUE! Are you kidding me?"

"Why what is wrong in that?" Roshan asked rubbing his head.

"It's ear nose and throat you idiot!" I explained.

"Oh shit! Why didn't you tell me?" He asked me.

"That's what I was doing you retard, I was pointing at my throat." I replied.

"No you pointed at your tongue!" Roshan argued.

"If I had to say tongue I would just stick it out you moron. Anyways I have to go now and I'm not going to fight with you on this stupid thing."

And I quickly packed my bag and left the room. Reena had called me home for the evening and I really had to go because there was something important that I needed to talk to her about. So I changed in the same department's bathroom into casuals and made my run to the auto stand.

Standing in front of her door I was talking to myself. "You have to tell her how you feel Himanshu. You can't just let it go on being friends with her like this. She needs to know how you feel!"

I took a deep breath and knocked on her door.

She opened the door and instead of a pretty face with a smile it was a sad one with her eyes flowing rivers. She almost fell into my arms hugging me really tight letting the rivers get flooded. We were still at the door and she wouldn't say anything or move. So I gently picked her up off her feet, stepped inside and closed the door behind. I took her to the couch and sat down with her still resting in my arms. I let her cry till she was drained out completely and all I could hear was sniffs and deep breaths. I pushed her face back and placed a kiss on her forehead.

"Now tell me what's wrong." I requested.

After a brief silence in her husky voice she said "My brother met an accident yesterday. My mom left last night itself to see him. I wanted to call you yesterday itself but you had an exam today, that's why I called you home today."

"Oh, how is he now?" I enquired.

"He is in the ICU in Bangalore. He has a broken arm and broken ribs but the doctors said he is out of danger now. I didn't know what to do Himanshu. I was so scared last night I couldn't even sleep. Can you please stay here tonight? I don't know what I would do if I were alone. Please don't go." She requested me.

"I'm not going anywhere alright. And your brother is also fine right? His arm would heal soon don't worry about that. Now tell me what do you want to order from dominos? I'm really hungry!" I changed the topic.

"Cheese burst!" She said with a small smile.

While we waited for the pizza guy she tried to enquire about why I ignored her the previous day at college.

"What was wrong with you yesterday?" She asked.

"What do you mean?" I asked hesitantly.

"You crossed me a total of four times in the college and you didn't even look at me. And the last time was too much. I even called out for you but you just kept walking away. Then I thought that you might be busy with your studies for the exam the next day so I didn't bother you." She elaborated.

"Really? I swear I didn't notice you yesterday. Wait I think the pizza guy is here. Let me check alright." I changed the topic successfully again.

The pizza had arrived and we sat on the floor and had it slowly but fought for the last slice. I let her win and take the slice but we ended up sharing it. When I gulped the last bite she smiled and said "There is something on your face."

"Where?" Rubbing my cheek I asked.

"Hmmm, let me."

She got herself on her knees and leaned forward towards me. She slowly came close to my face and rested her left hand on my right shoulder. She gently held my face in her right hand and pulled it up. She brought her lips closer to mine and then slowly licked off the cheese which was stuck next to my lips. Suddenly I realized that it had been weeks since we had known each other and we never even had our first kiss. But this wasn't the best time. I had thought about opening up to her tonight and telling her the truth but that was definitely not going to happen tonight. So I held her by her arms and gently pushed her back.

"So where am I going to sleep?" I asked.

"In the bedroom!" She replied.

"And where are you going to sleep?" I asked again.

"In the bedroom!" She replied again.

"You are talking about two different bedrooms right?" I asked.

"Let's find out!" She said with a smile.

She grabbed my hand and pulled me up. She got behind me and closed my eyes and pushed me forwards to the bedroom. At the door of the bedroom she let me open my eyes and said "This is where you sleep!"

"And what about you?" I enquired.

She again put her hands in front of my eyes removing it in a few seconds and said "Here!"

We were still standing at the same bedroom door and I understood what she was trying to imply but for some reason I was uncomfortable. Usually when a pretty girl invites me to her bedroom to sleep with her I would jump on to the bed without thinking about it, but tonight I had a reason to keep myself from being me, but there was nothing much that I could have done.

"Aren't you going to carry me to our bed?" She asked with a naughty smile.

I swept her off her feet and she put her arms around my shoulders. I walked to the bed and placed her down. She didn't let go of me and pulled me in. I was lying on top of her when she started unbuttoning my shirt.

"Reena, may be this isn't the best idea." I suggested.

She stopped for a second and left my shirt.

"What isn't a good idea?" She asked in a disappointed voice.

I kept quiet. She then grabbed my collar and pulled me closer. My lips almost touched hers and I could feel her breath on my lips.

"Where is my kiss?" She asked in whispers.

I closed my eyes, leaned forward and let our lips meet. Soon the kiss turned into a smooch and we rolled over for her to get on top. She pulled my shirt open still smooching me hard while I held her hips. I could foresee where we would conclude eventually and so I had to do something. I slowly slid my hands down and pinched her hard on her ass.

"Ouch! Why would you do that? You know how much of a turn off that is for me?" She almost screamed and got off me. She was about to get off the bed when I pulled her back into my arms and hugged her tight so that we could face the same direction.

"Let's just take it slow alright. How about we just snuggle up tight and sleep together?" I whispered in her ears.

She hummed in agreement and I hugged her tighter. Soon she drove into her dreams but I could not. I was glad we didn't do anything more but still the blame was mine. After cursing myself this way for a while I closed my eyes.

Her brother took three weeks to get discharged from the hospital and till then most of our conversations were about the same topic. Soon her final exams started and all I was supposed to do was to console her and push her to her books. The feelings and emotions I had inside my heart were too strong but I couldn't have told her about any of it during her exams. I had not felt this way about anyone in a long time and it was very difficult for me to not let her know. During the same time even I had my semester exams but more importantly I was eagerly waiting for her exams to get over so that I could tell her how exactly I felt.

On the same day her exams got over, she left to Dubai with her mom as she had four weeks of holidays. And I was left here alone with my feelings which were very difficult to handle. I never got a good chance to tell her and the pain and struggle that I was going through was too much to handle. I started bunking more classes and having sleepless nights. Even though my performance was going down in most of the subjects, the professor who came to class this Monday surprised not just me but every single person in class.

Dr Kamal, who was given the nick name "Penguin" because of his walk, got in the class room and took the mic. As usual I was sitting amongst the last few rows trying to find a cosy place to sleep. I hid behind Rajesh who was the only other guy in class as big as me who could hide me behind himself. I still couldn't stop thinking about the way my life was screwed up right now. Reena wasn't here yet and I had to tell her how I felt. It was driving me insane.

"Before we start the class today I want to talk to all of you about the semester exam that happened last week. I have to say most of you performed fairly

169

badly. I did not expect distinctions from this batch but when I found out that only 7 out of 120 students have passed I was surprised. When we asked you to write a short note on the topic "Dry Day" we did not ask you to mention 15th August, 26th January and 2nd October. Dry day was not in context with alcohol. At first I was fine with finding such an answer in the boy's answer sheets but I was very shocked to find out that some of you girls knew those dates very well too. Well dry day isn't about alcohol; it's about keeping the area around your house and your locality dry, to avoid stagnant water so that mosquitoes don't breed in such areas. And only 7 students who have passed wrote the answers correctly. And I'm surprised that this number of 7 comprises of a boy as well. "

Everyone's eyes turned to Suraj who was known to be the highest scorer in boys all the time. When that announcement was made Suraj was so confident that he crossed his arms and leaned back on the backrest of his chair as if he had won a gold medal in community medicine. The professor then continued.

"I was told not to mention the names in class like this but I just cannot resist myself to appreciate these people who have done so well. And I hope next time all of you will work hard to get your names in this list. The highest scorer is Shalini, followed by Rakhi, Shruti, Anitha, Amrita and Natasha. And the last but not the least the only boy who managed to just crawl across the pass marks was Himanshu. His answers weren't that good but they were very well written. I hope to see not 7 but 70 names in the next exams ok. Now let us start the class."

The second I heard my name I was dumbstruck. I had failed in the other two subjects and I had written this paper equally bad. I had no idea how they could have passed me. I guess I knew how to bull shit in the answers. The second Kamal sir turned towards the screen to start the class, Rajesh turned around and hit me hard with his textbook on my shoulder.

"Dude relax I have no idea how that happened." I tried to justify.

"I'll see you after class. I'm not done with you yet." Rajesh said angrily.

During the entire class I got many stares from a lot of people, especially Suraj. Soon the class was over and Dr. Kamal was directing his waggling feet out of the class room. The second he stepped out of the class I was surrounded by few boys who started hitting me left and right.

"Guys stop; I don't know how I passed ok." I tried to save my ass.

"May be they switched his paper with someone else's like it happened in first year!" Suraj said in his wicked voice.

"Probably that happened." I said hoping the beating would stop.

I was almost dragged down to the community medicine department with Suraj Rajesh and BD, to check out if I really did well. I went in and requested Kamal sir to let me have a look at my paper. I took my answer sheet from him and stepped out. The next second the answer sheet was snatched away by Suraj and all three of them started going through my paper. After few minutes BD and Rajesh gave up but Suraj kept flipping the pages with a surprised expression on his face.

My phone buzzed for a text and I took it out. It was Reena's text which read "Cn u meet me nw, in the juice stal?"

"Whn did u come bak? Evn I hv sumthin very important to tel u! Wil b thr in 5!" I replied.

"Let it go Suraj, maybe he did write well, we all know he can write stories pretty well." BD told Suraj.

"Hey guys I have to go now. And Suraj please return the paper to Kamal sir when you are satisfied ok."

I quickly ran out and took the stairs. I was a bit surprised as there was still a week for Reena's results to come out and she was back already. I almost ran to the juice stall and found her sitting alone in one corner. She did not look very pretty.

"Hey, when did you come back?" I asked Reena.

"This afternoon!" She replied.

"How come, I thought your results were coming out next week?" I enquired.

"They have called back all the ones who have failed so that if we want we can submit our applications for re-evaluation." She explained.

I was surprised, rather shocked. I mean she wasn't that bright of a student but she wasn't so bad that she would fail.

"So did you submit the application?" I asked.

While she nodded her head tears rolled down her eyes. Some people on the next tables gave me a "you did it again Himanshu" stares but I ignored them and focused on Reena as she needed me at that moment.

"Why are you crying Reena? Don't worry; you are going to make it through the re-evaluation. Trust me!" I tried to comfort her.

"That's not the only reason I'm crying Himanshu." She replied.

"I'm all ears to you now; tell me Reena, what's wrong?" I asked.

"Can we please get out of here? I don't want to talk about it here; I won't be able to control myself." She replied almost losing control of her tears.

I got up and held her by her hands to walk to the auto stand. We drove directly to her house. She broke down into tears on the elevator itself and I had to control her. I took out the keys from her purse and we sat down on the same couch where she cried on my shoulders a couple of months ago.

"Listen Reena, you are going to do fine in the re-evaluation ok." I tried to console her.

"That isn't what is bothering me so much Himanshu!" She explained.

"Then what is it Reena? Tell me!" I asked anxiously.

"When I was at home I heard my parents fought a lot of times. There were many times when I tried to ask them about it but they would just ignore me. My dad wasn't even there at home most of the nights. He used to come back from work, fight with mom and then just leave. And then on the day I was about to leave for India, they both came and sat me down in front of them. I was really scared and then mom started speaking. She told me how things were not working between them and they are considering a divorce. I was shattered Himanshu. I just sat there and started weeping. My dad yelled at me to grow up and face life practically and just left. Mom hugged me said that everything will be alright. Dad didn't even come to drop me at the airport. He didn't even care about me failing in my exams. Tell me Himanshu, how are things going to be ok? I don't want them to split, I love them both and I don't know what to do." She said with many breaks gasping for breath and crying many times.

"Reena that is something you cannot do anything about alright. Just don't think about it. Let them handle it. I'm sure they will conclude with something that is better for all of you." I tried to console her.

"I hope things get better Himanshu; I'm already going through so much of shit!" She said wiping her tears off her cheeks.

I didn't know what else to say so I just held her strong and hugged her.

"Wait, you told me that you had something important to tell me. Did you find another girl when I wasn't here?" She wiped her tears away and said winking at me.

For a second I was surprised, and then I wished I could tell her what's going in my head. I really wished I could but I just couldn't. Not at this time. I cursed my life for being so complicated. Why did I even have to get into a situation like this? Why couldn't I just tell her the truth about how I felt and get it over with?

"Himanshu is something bothering you?" She asked again.

"No Reena, I'm perfectly fine." I replied.

"Are you sure?" She insisted.

"Yes Reena!" I answered.

"Can I ask you something?"

"Sure!" I nodded to Reena.

"Would you stay back with me tonight if you don't mind?" She requested.

"Reena I have to get back to the hostel. And if I get caught I might get into a lot of trouble!" I was giving excuses.

"Please Himanshu; I really need to be not alone right now. Please?" She pleaded this time.

"Do you really need me to stay?" I asked.

"Yes!" She replied.

"Fine I'll stay. But on one condition!" I asked.

"What is that?" She was curious.

"You are not going to molest me!" I put forward my condition.

"Well I cannot guarantee that!" She said winking at me and led me to the bed room.

Chapter Seventeen

"PUSH IT HARDER"

Reena's re-evaluation results were due in a week's time and that week was full of tension and anxiousness for both of us. For her because it was her results and for me because I really wanted to open up to her and tell her everything. Finally the day had come and I was near the office where they would put up the results on the notice board even before anyone else had come. The peon came and stuck the notice on the board. I started searching for her name but I couldn't find it. There were 6 names and none of them was Reena. I checked again but the name wasn't there. And then I looked at the title of the notice and realized the names were only of those people who couldn't make it even after the re-evaluation. That meant that Reena had cleared. I was so glad for Reena had passed, but even more so for I could tell her everything now.

I skipped my lunch and my class and went straight to Reena's house. Well I went down there not just to tell her about the results but because I desperately needed to talk to her. I knew that if I open up to her about everything she would be surprised but I just had to tell her everything. I ran up the stairs of her apartment and knocked on her door.

"Yes?" An old lady who opened the door enquired.

"Is Reena here?" I enquired.

"Yes, may I know who you are?" She asked.

"Himanshu, her friend!"

"Oh yes, please come in. She is in her room. Why don't you go meet her there?" She suggested.

"Oh ok. Thanks aunty." I replied.

I walked straight to her bedroom. I'm sure her mom would have wondered how I knew the way around the house so well. I knocked on her bedroom door and opened it.

"I don't want to talk to any one right now. Please leave me alone!" She screamed burying her face in to the pillow.

"Reena it's me!" I said.

"Himanshu? When did you come? I'm sorry; I didn't know it was you." She responded.

"No that's alright but why are you so angry? Wait, have you been crying all day?" I asked her.

She took a leap forward and hugged me and the rivers started again. I wanted to bang my head on the wall at this moment. Why does God do this to me? Why is it that every time I have to open up to her, something or the other has to go wrong with her? Somehow I controlled my emotions as I had a river to stop.

"Reena control yourself! Tell me what happened now?" I requested her.

"Mom came back today morning." She told me.

"So you should be happy no?" I asked.

"But dad isn't coming!" She continued.

"That's ok. Maybe he got stuck with some work. I'm sure he'll come as soon as he can." I assumed and told her so.

"No Himanshu, he isn't coming. Ever!" She almost cried again while telling me.

I kept quiet as I just didn't know what to say. Moreover I was busy cursing my luck inside my head.

"Himanshu why does this happen to me? Why does my life have to be so complicated? Why can't it be simple like everybody else's?" She asked me.

And I asked myself the same question!

After a while I realized her mom was also in the house. I could not just sit on her bed hugging her really tight while she was in her night gown. I actually didn't even notice that she was in her night gown till now and how pretty she was looking.

"Reena, your mom is outside. Maybe we should go and sit outside." I suggested.

"I don't want to go anywhere Himanshu. I wish I could just run away from all this. I don't want to face my mom or my dad again. I'm going back to the hostel tomorrow. And I'm going to stay there the rest of the year." She told me.

"Oh ok. May be I should get going now. It's getting late." I replied.

"Ok. Text me once you reach the hostel ok. I'll see you in college tomorrow." She responded.

"Ok." Smiling at her I got off the bed to leave.

"Hey Himanshu?"

"Yeah!"

"I love you!" She confessed with a smile.

I leaned towards her and placed a kiss on her forehead. And then making a mess of her hair I bid goodbye to her.

I was so stuck up with the whole Reena issue that I had not even paid attention to my academic performances recently. Our last posting before the final exams of third year was in the OBG department, and had started 2 weeks ago and I hadn't even attended a single delivery. So this time I decided to go to the labour room and actually find out why the women screamed so much while pushing their babies out. Once we were done giving the attendance we entered the labour room all set to watch some new babies popping out. There were three delivery rooms and we heard screams of different tone and pitches from each of them. Frankly speaking I was a little scared to enter any one of them. I had read about a normal delivery and all the gluey stuff that follows. I mean watching blood and intestines was fine with me somehow but I just couldn't picture a delivery. Even though I wasn't ready my friends dragged me along and pushed me to stand right behind the professor who was conducting the delivery. From this place I could watch the entire procedure properly, though I wish I wasn't in this place. The patient was a 34 year old lady who was having her 6th child. Given the age it wasn't a very pleasing view from where I was standing. She kept screaming louder and louder. Every time the patient screamed in pain, the professor would scream louder at her to push. The screaming continued and the pushing kept going and suddenly I could see a small head popping out. The lady screamed more and pushed harder and the head of the baby was out. I was standing there with my mouth wide open to see the entire baby being pulled out of the mother. The professor clamped and cut the cord and gave the baby to the nurse standing next to her and then focused back on the exit hole. That is when I found that the ugly part of a delivery was after the baby was born.

"The placenta seems adherent, I will manually detach it." Saying this she stuck one of her hands into the patient's vagina while she manipulated her abdomen with the other. I almost puked and wanted to leave the room that second. I turned around to realize a bunch of my batch mates standing and staring at the entire procedure, especially the girls. I couldn't find a way out and had to stay and witness the happenings.

"I got it." Suddenly the professor exclaimed and pulled out a bag which looked like it was full of poop. That was the placenta. After examining it she threw it down in a small tub which was next to my feet. The gluey stuff splashed and stained my pants. I was already feeling nauseous and when I looked down to see my pants, everything seemed so blurry. I looked back up and all I could see was a flash of light and then darkness. I woke up few hours later in the casualty with an IV line on my right hand. BD was sitting next to me and got up realizing I was back to my senses.

"Finally the great doctor has woken up from his sleep. So how do you feel now sir?" BD taunted me.

"What happened dude? Why am I here?" I enquired.

"You fainted and collapsed after that delivery, remember?" He tried to explain.

"I didn't faint dude. That gluey stuff was all over the floor and I slipped." I was only trying to not make myself look like a fool.

"Oh is that why you fell forwards on the professor and almost smashed her face on to you know where?" BD elaborated.

"What? I fell on her?" I was embarrassed.

"Yup and your batch mates had to jump in to pull you back up. You were totally out man. They brought you here and called me. It has been more than 4 hours that you have been sleeping." BD explained the entire story.

I didn't know what else to say and started looking here and there to avoid eye contact with him. Suddenly I noticed a pair of legs wearing the same uniform pants hiding behind the curtain on the next bed.

"Is some other student also admitted here for something?" I asked BD.

"No, not just one but three of you boys fainted during that delivery. But fortunately you were the first and the only one who fell on the professor." He said with a giant laughter.

"Fine fine. Now get me out of here." I requested BD.

BD finished the formalities and we were out of the casualty in no time. While walking to the hostel we both discussed how we actually had to start studying now as our final exams were approaching.

It had been over a month that the divorce news was broken to Reena. She seemed to be coping well with the whole situation and even better, she was dealing with the second year much better than how I did. And the thoughts of me opening up to her started bothering me again. So just like any other day I asked her to meet me at the juice stall after classes.

"Hey, so what was this important thing you wanted to talk to me about?" She asked placing herself on the seat opposite to me.

"Let us order something to eat first? I'm hungry!" I declared.

We both got our orders and sat in front of each other.

"So tell me how your day was?" I enquired.

"It was ok. That Brigadier Philip tried really hard to tell us how to take a case history but we disappointed him like always. It was fun though. How was your day?" She asked.

"Yeah it was ok." I replied.

This way our conversation kept going on and on for over an hour when she realized it was time for her to go back to the hostel. At many times I tried to tell her how I felt but I just couldn't bring myself up to tell her on her face. I was really scared. So I thought maybe I'll confess to her over the phone and requested her to call me around 8 pm.

I walked back to the hostel in despair thinking about the whole thing. How can I tell her the entire thing? Will she understand? What if she doesn't? All these thoughts ran away when I heard my phone ringing. I checked my watch to learn it was only 7 pm. Why was Reena calling me so early?

"Hello?"

"Why did you do this to me Himanshu? Did I ever hurt you or cause you any trouble. Then why did you have to do this to me? My life was already so messed up, and I was leaning on you. All I wanted was a little bit of support and you had to hurt me like this. Why Himanshu why? What pleasure did you get in hurting me like this? Was I not good enough for you? Didn't I give in to you? Then why Himanshu? Tell me Himanshu, tell me why!"

Not even a single word was coming to my head that I could say to justify myself. I was shocked and cursing myself.

"You go behind my back and hurt me like this. And you don't even have the courtesy to justify yourself? I looked at you as a good friend who would never hurt me. Now I wish I had never met you. I hate you Himanshu, I hate you to the core." And the phone got cut.

I moved the phone away from my ears and started typing in a number to make a call. But before I could hit the green button, my phone rang again.

"Listen to me Aditi, let me explain, please." I answered the call.

"No Mr Himanshu, you listen to me. I thought of you as the perfect guy I could have found. I overlooked all your flaws and changed myself for you, to make you like me better. I fell for you. I loved you. I thought there could not have been a better guy for me. And you proved me wrong. How stupid of me to actually let my shell open and let you in. Guys are all born jerks aren't they? And I thought you were different. You are not different at all. You are just one among those cold hearted bastards Himanshu."

"Aditi please listen to me."

"Tell me Himanshu, did you have enough fun with me? And when was it that you were going to dump me and find yourself another prey? Oh wait, you must be unhappy with me right, for I didn't let you have sex with me even though we spent a night together. I'm glad I didn't do anything stupid with you. You are such a jerk Himanshu."

My eyes were draining all the fluid out from my body when I heard a sniff from the other side of the phone.

"I loved you truly Himanshu, and I gave you everything I could have. I did everything from my side possible. And even then you chose somebody over me. Tell me Himanshu, wasn't I good enough for you? Was I not worth it?"

"No Aditi, please let me explain please."

"No Himanshu I don't want to hear anything anymore. I have had enough. Even when my friend told me about Reena I tried to argue and disagree. But when I called the hostel and spoke to Reena myself, I was shocked. I couldn't believe that my Himanshu could do this to me. You stepped right into my heart Himanshu and burned it down. There is nothing left in my chest anymore. I will never be able to love again. I will never see to life as I did before. All thanks to you.

"Aditi please."

"No Himanshu. I'm done with you. I hate you. Don't call me ever again. Don't even bother to contact me in anyway. But learn one thing Himanshu, you will never find true love in your life. Remember my words."

The phone got disconnected and my eyes lost their control.

Chapter Eighteen

"LET US GO BACK IN TIME, AGAIN"

I was frustrated and tired and all I wanted was to get away from Neha as far away as possible. After reaching my room the only thing I remember was a glimpse of my bed and then BD poking me with my badminton racket the next morning. He used to use the racket as a protective shield in case I turn violent after waking up.

"Himanshu get up, we have a meeting now." BD told me.

"What meeting?" I asked.

"Arts festival is coming up in a month and we have to start practicing man." He replied.

"Where is it?" I asked again.

"In the mess hall!" He responded.

"When is it?" I asked again.

"Right now!!" He almost screamed.

"Fine I'll be there in some time, you go ahead." I replied calmly.

BD left the room and I got up picking up my phone. There were many more texts from Neha which I deleted without even reading it. There was one more message from an unknown number that read "hey u! hows it going? Its been 4evr hasn't it? yup its been 4evr! ;)"

As it was from an unknown number I ignored it. I quickly freshened up and rushed to the mess hall to join the meeting in progress.

"Himanshu, thank God you are here. You are in charge of the dance group. Pick on the people and the songs and start the practice soon. And don't worry about the props and costumes; we'll help you with all that later ok." Our class rep told me.

"Is that it?" BD who was sitting close by took a glance at me and I flipped him off for making me get up and come all this way for something I knew already.

I took a lazy walk back to my room and I checked my phone. It had another message from the same unknown number.

"Do u generally ignore people like dis or is it jst me?"

This time instead of replying I decided to call that number.

"Hello?" said a very subtle calm and sweet voice.

"Hey, do I know you?" In a surprised voice I asked.

"I'm sure you do." Came the response.

"Ok, do you mind telling me who you are? And why exactly are you texting me?" I enquired.

"Because I wanted to talk to you!" The sweet voice justified.

"And why is that?" I asked further.

"Don't tell me that you haven't had any of your fans calling you up like this?" The blissful voice said with a giggle.

"In fact I have never had a girl with such a sweet voice call me when she doesn't know me. Moreover if I knew you I'm sure I would have been good friends with you by now. So tell me who you are!" I requested.

"This is Shivani!"

"You actually want me to believe that! I don't know any one named Shivani!" I replied.

"It's not my fault you don't know me. But I know you very well." Shivani said.

By this time I was sure it was probably one of my friends playing a prank on me. I mean I never get this lucky, a girl calling me wanting to talk to me like this. That is something that would have never happened to me.

"Listen Miss Shivani or whoever you are, if you are not going to tell me who you are then I'm just going to keep the phone." I threatened her.

"Why are you getting so angry? My name is Shivani!" She insisted.

This was when I got a text from Roshika and I had to end the conversation with Shivani.

"Listen whoever you are; I'm not falling for this trick ok. I have to go now but whoever told you to play this prank on me, tell him or her that I am not falling for it!" And I kept the phone.

I was very certain that it was a prank. I kept getting texts from the same number later that day. At first I completely ignored them but later when she apologized via texts we started having chats often. That entire Sunday I was mostly busy replying to her texts. Even though I had a major issue bothering me that day, Shivani got my attention. She seemed to be a very nice girl, with a very peaceful and calming voice and for once a girl who spoke to me had a good control over her language and humour.

185

Even though I knew Shivani wasn't her real name, it didn't happen very often that I liked a girl for her voice, language and humour without even knowing how she looks or has any assets. I was sure to learn more about this girl soon.

That same day I had learned about Neha messing up things for me and for some reason I opened up to Shivani about everything over the next few days. There was this calm in her voice that used to make me want to talk to her more. May be the reason that I had never met her was the reason why I was so comfortable talking to her. She was the one who convinced me to go up and confront Neha regarding things which was probably the best I could do at that time compared to my idea of just letting it go and take things lightly. It had been just few days since I started talking to her and I had started to feel dependent on her already.

During this time I had also met Reena and even though she was pretty and I had never even seen Shivani, I was leaning more towards Shivani as I really loved the amazing person that she was. She used to understand my emotions even before I put them into words. She use to guide me through the situations I used to face in college, she used to push me to study as my exams were nearing. She was slowly bringing faith back into my heart and taught me how to love again. I had almost fallen for her when something went wrong and I blamed it entirely on my freaking bad luck.

Even though I and Shivani had it going wonderful for over a month now, one day suddenly her phone was switched off. I kept trying her number over and over again but it just wouldn't ring. None of the messages got delivered and I did not hear from her for more than a month. I started believing that I'm just not meant to find a girl who would actually like me for what I am. I figured that I might have done something wrong that made her run away from me. I didn't even know her real name so there was no way I could have traced her. So I let it go.

Meanwhile Reena seemed to be the only other person I could depend on. She wasn't as mature and dependable but her company was better than being alone. Moreover she liked me too. So this thing between us caught fire in no time. I got done with my exams and started talking to her very often. There was no doubt she was falling for me or rather had fallen for me already. I wasn't so sure about falling for her and the day I actually decided to sit down and think about considering Reena seriously, something shocking happened that made sure that nothing could happen between me and Reena.

I just met Reena at the juice stall and got back to the hostel. I changed and sat down with my ear phones on ready to give this whole thing a serious thought. Before I could start my thought process my phone rang. It wasn't Reena. It was Shivani!

"Hello?" I said in a surprised shivering voice.

"Hey, please don't yell at me, I have a valid reason." Shivani replied.

"What is it?" I said changing my tone from softness to anger.

"My dad learned that my Passport was going to expire soon and so I had to hurry up and leave for US within 2 days. I had to apply for leave at my college as well and I just couldn't find time to inform you. And then when I got back I had my exams and had to study a lot. Today was my last exam and the second I got out of the exam hall I called you. I'm so sorry Himanshu."

"Well sorry isn't enough this time." I said.

"Please Himanshu I'm really sorry. Isn't there anything that I can do to make it up to you? Please?" She pleaded.

"Nope. There is nothing that you can do!" I replied sternly.

"So you are not going to talk to me ever again?" She asked softly.

"Nope!" I was being rude.

"Not even if I tell you my real name?" She tempted me.

"What? Oh tell me already!" I was curious.

"Nope." Now she was playing with me.

"This isn't fair, I'm the one who should be angry and not talk to you. You cannot give me conditions like this!" I reacted.

"Promise me that you wouldn't quit on me and I'll tell you my real name." She told me her condition.

"No I don't want to talk to you." I declared.

"Fine then goodbye!" She replied.

"Ok fine I promise I won't stop talking to you. Alright?" I was melting down.

"Aditi, and I'm doing 2nd year in architecture from Kochi University! So tell me how you have been for the last two months without me?" She asked.

"I'm still angry with you!" I responded.

"What? But why? Aditi is my real name I promise." I explained.

"You lied to me about your name, how can I trust you?" I questioned her.

"I'm really sorry about that too but I wasn't sure if I should tell you my real name in the beginning. It was supposed to be a prank remember?" She said in a chirpy voice.

"And who asked you to play this prank on me?" I asked.

"Promise me you wouldn't go and ask her regarding this?" She again put forward a condition.

"Fine I wouldn't! Tell me now." I agreed.

"Remember Swapna, your Christmas friend? You made her run in class and tie pony tails?" She asked.

"Yeah I do. She asked you to play a prank on me?" I enquired.

"Yeah she did, but that was long ago and I had denied at first. Then that day I was really bored and I still had your number so for fun I texted you. But please don't go and ask her about this now." She explained.

"Fine but I'm still not talking to you!" I said.

"Can I do anything to make you talk to me?" She enquired politely.

"Meet me!" I put a condition for the first time.

"As in person?" She asked.

"Yes!" I replied.

"Barista on marine drives tomorrow at 5 pm?" She said.

"Really?" I was surprised.

"Yup, I wouldn't want to lose such an awesome friend now would I?" She agreed.

"Hmmm, so did you get your passport renewed?" I asked.

"Yes I did." She replied.

"And how were your exams?"

This way our conversation went on for hours and hours together. Of what I remember we were talking about her interest in singing and poetry and then I heard my phone ring again!

"Hello?" I asked in a cranky voice.

"Get up Himanshu! Otherwise you'll get late for college!" She almost yelled at me.

"Did I sleep off while talking to you last night?" I asked Aditi.

"Yes you did! We spoke till 4 in the morning so I don't blame you. I'm still in my jet lag phase so I was wide awake. We'll talk when you get back from college if I'm awake. But for now get yourself off your bed and get going." She almost ordered me.

"Fine! I'll call you once I'm back alright!" I replied.

I rushed to college and barely made it to my ENT posting. It was a day before the end posting exam and I had studied nothing. All my friends were making plans to sit down from five in the evening together and study for the exam. But I had some other plans at 5. I had to meet Shivani. I mean Aditi.

     As soon as the class got over at 4 pm I ran down the stairs to the auto stand. Marine drive was a distance of about 10 kilometres so I had to hurry up. On the way I crossed Reena and in the last 24 hours this was the first time that her thought crossed my mind only after she came in front of me. She was walking straight towards me and she had seen me. If I stayed back and spoke to her I would have gotten late so I decided to ignore her and walked past her in a hurry. I almost ran to the auto stand and got in to one in a hurry and asked for marine drives without even bargaining. After a drive of 20 minutes I reached the venue. I was still in my uniform so I went straight to the wash room of Barista and changed into something more decent. I set my hair up with some hair gel and left the top two buttons of my shirt open. I walked out to still find all the tables empty and myself 15 minutes ahead of schedule. I was glad I had reached before her but the bad part now was the wait.

I sat in one corner table waiting for her. Many people walked in and out of Barista in the next 15 minutes. First came in a tall pretty girl who I thought was Aditi. Long slender legs wrapped in denim, a tight t-shirt with a small purse hanging by the side and a high pony tail, this girl sure did make a first impression. But while she was placing her order at the counter a guy came from behind and rested his arm on this girl's shoulder. So I concluded her as not Aditi. Next came in a group of people, both guys and girls. They were all dressed in jeans and t-shirts but the girl who entered at the end stood apart from the crowd. She was wearing a regular salwar suit. She was looking around as if she was waiting for somebody, probably me! But Aditi was from US and she wasn't going to dress up like that if she had to come meet me, I was pretty sure about that. This girl continued to look around for a while and then decided to come and sit 2 tables away from me. While she walked closer I realized how pretty she was. The simplicity and soberness of her attire had an appeal. Her netted sky blue coloured dupatta hanging down from her shoulders increased the beauty of her white kurta which was in contrast to her dark blue leggings. Her white flat sandals did not raise her higher but surely raised her appearance. The open hair was blowing away with the softest of the breeze from the air conditioner close by exposing the long dangling ear rings that she was wearing. She had big beautiful eyes that had locked mine on to themselves. She didn't have any big assets but those subtle curves did grab my attention for a second.

"What are you doing Himanshu? For now focus! You are here to meet Aditi and no matter how badly you want to talk to this pretty lady next to you, you just can't! What if Aditi walks in and finds you eyeing on this girl? Your love story is dead before it's born. So just relax and try not to think of anything." I said to myself.

I tried to focus on the door ahead of me. Soon a girl dressed in a short mid-thigh length black silky skirt and a white shirt walked in. She definitely did have a classy choice of clothes. More over the skirt was hugging her really tight accurately showing the acute angles of her curves. Even though the shirt was loose, the top most buttons which were open were a proof that a lot of air was required over there. Her hair was tied with a crunchy and she was wearing red lipstick. Even though lipstick girls weren't my thing but it did suit her. I did like her from her first step into Barista. She went to the counter, asked for something and then came and sat next to my table between me and the girl in the white salwar. She sat down and took her phone out and dialled a number. The next second my phone rang and my target was set. I picked up and heard her voice saying hello in coordination with those lips painted in red lipstick. I turned to her side and said "Aditi?"

I was completely turned towards her. It almost looked like I was sitting on her table and not mine. My eyes were totally set on her face and there was nothing else in the picture.

"Excuse me?" She replied.

That response did surprise me. I was totally confused when a second face popped in. The girl in the salwar slowly leaned forwards and her face emerged into the picture.

"Himanshu?" She asked.

I quickly got up from my table and sat on Aditi's after apologizing to the girl in the black skirt!

"You almost got me beaten up there." I gestured at the girl in the black skirt and told Aditi.

"What? How? I didn't ask you to go and talk to that girl who looks like a total . . . ! Anyways so you don't like me dressing up in such kind of dresses?" She asked.

"No nothing like that. I'm glad this is you and not her." I responded.

"Why what's wrong with her? Why can't I be like her?" She was teasing me.

"You want to be like her?" I was surprised.

"Actually no I don't." She said with a giggle.

"Can we not talk about her? I think she can hear us!" I whispered leaning forwards.

She also leaned forward and whispered to me "So what do you want to talk about?"

I leaned back on my chair and smiled. I didn't have words to describe how cute she was. She stepped right into my heart. Till now I was only wondering if I was going to fall for her but now I was sure that I had already fallen for her. Aditi was just magical!

We spoke and laughed together and time drove past us in full throttle. It was more than two hours since we had been there and it was time for her to get back to her hostel. I paid the bill and we stood up to leave. She took a few quick steps to make her feet walk with mine. She slowly grabbed my hand into hers and we walked out of Barista hand in hand. We walked to the auto stand and before she got into one I turned her to face me. I held both her hands in mine and prepared myself to speak.

"No one has ever made such a big impact on me in the first meet. I hope you know how pretty you are!" I spoke.

She just smiled and I realized how much prettier she looks with that smile. I don't know what happened to me suddenly but I leaned forwards and pecked her on her lips.

When I moved back her eyes were still closed for a second. Before her eyes opened her lips widened and that smile came back on. She confessed she really likes me and then got in to the auto with a blush.

"Text me as soon as you reach the hostel" I almost screamed as her auto sped away from me.

As soon as I got back to the hostel I opened up my book and started studying for the exam the next day. It was a small ENT end posting exam, not that big of a deal. After the exam Reena had called me home. I hadn't thought about her in days ever since Aditi was back. Clearly I was into Aditi and not her. I had to tell her. I and Reena had not started off that way yet and I was hoping I would be able to end it right here. So with my mind all set to confess to Reena I decided to go to her house. But the situation wasn't that easy. Her brother had just met an accident and Reena was in tears when I reached her flat. She needed me as a good friend now and she was too vulnerable. I could not have told her about Aditi yet. I had to wait. I had to let go of my confession for now and wait for things to settle down and look for a better opportunity. I was stuck between the two girls, one who I needed and the one who needed me.

Chapter Nineteen

"THE PERFECT DATE"

Days went on and I met Aditi several more times. Every single time I saw her I realized how much more I was falling for her. But the constant thought of Reena used to bother me a lot. Soon Reena's exams started and there was no way I could have broken her heart right now. She got busy with her books and I got to spend more time with Aditi. We had both understood that we needed to spend more time together in person apart from those couple of hours we used to get just before she needed to get back to the hostel from college. So we discussed and decided to stay over at a hotel for the weekend. It was a huge step that we were going to take. She had never been with a guy before and I was her first one. The responsibility on me to not screw up anything was too much. But I had to stand up for it.

I had to pick up Aditi from her college at 4. I was standing there with my back pack waiting for her. I had booked a beach resort for the weekend. I had to make it special for her for she was so special for me.

"What are you waiting for? Shall we go?" The calm voice of Aditi breezed my ears.

I was so lost in my thoughts I didn't realize when she came and stood next to me.

"Auto?" I screamed!

"Hey, can we walk for a little while?" She requested.

"Sure." I replied pulling her hand into mine.

I gestured the auto guy to go on and held her hand before she could think about it. She told me about her day at college and how her architecture professors were so boring and I agreed that it is the same case in every college. We walked the footpath hand in hand for a little while and then she confessed she was tired of walking and wanted to go to the place where we were going to stay. I waved a hand for the auto passing by and he stopped. "Cherai beach resort" I ordered and he started driving. It was a 20 minutes' drive and during the first half of it there was nothing but silence between the two of us.

"Are you scared?" To break the silence she asked.

"No. Why should I be scared?" I replied.

"What if we get caught or if something goes wrong?" She asked.

"No I'm not." I was stern and confident.

"Well I am!" She confessed in a shivering voice.

"Aditi, I wouldn't let anything go wrong. Don't worry ok." And I slowly raised my arm around her head and rested it on her shoulder.

"So where are we going?" She asked.

"You'll know soon. But I was wondering why you didn't get any bags." I enquired.

"I got my back pack no?" She replied.

"You are a girl Aditi, just one bag is enough for you?" I asked surprisingly.

"We are staying for just one night no? Why would I need a lot of luggage for that?" She responded.

I smiled looking at her and learned that every little thing about her was perfect. She wasn't a regular girl and that was something I loved about her. Soon we reached the resort and we exited the auto.

"Himanshu this place looks very expensive." She said surprisingly.

"Don't worry about that. Let's go in." I pulled her forwards.

We walked in to the reception area. Even though I offered to carry her bag myself she didn't let me. She looked scared. Her eyes were getting bigger with every step we took towards the hotel. Her legs were almost shivering and her gait wasn't very straight. She was holding my arm strong and I felt good that she was depending on me. I had already made the reservation so the formality at the desk did not take much time. A luggage boy took both our bags and directed us towards our villa. She was right about the place being very expensive. Even though I wanted to make it very special for her I could not arrange a lot of money and had to manage with a small double bedded villa which was one of the cheaper ones on the list. There were suites and better villas but I didn't have enough money for all that. The luggage boy opened the door for us, dropped the bags on a table in the room and left without asking for a tip. We got in and I realized even I was getting scared a little. This was the first time I was staying over with a girl in a hotel. For the fact that she was scared too, I couldn't have showed my fear and so I broke the silence.

"Hey if you want to change, go ahead and hurry up, the sun will set soon and I don't want to miss that."

"No I think I'm fine." She replied.

"Ok then let's go." And I grabbed her hand and pulled her out of the room.

"Wait; let me leave my sandals here."

I was standing at the door waiting for her. She took few steps towards me, raised herself on her toes and pecked me on my cheeks. My smile got widened and for a second I was dumbstruck.

"Let's go now!" She exclaimed.

I nodded in agreement and we walked to the beach. Walking on the sand with her hand in mine and our naked feet was a blissful feeling. It was so movie like but I loved the feeling. I walked all the way to the water and dipped my feet in it. At first she resisted to get in the water but soon she jumped in too. We both stood next to each other and checked if the water could carry away the sand from under us. And when it did not happen she started splashing water at me. Even though we were splashing water on each other I had to be sure not to overdo it. She was wearing a yellow top and if it got wet it would become see through. So even though I wanted to pick her up and throw her in the water I controlled my feelings.

The beach was a private property of the hotel so there were not many people around. Once we were done playing with the water we both wanted to find a cosy spot to sit down together. I pulled her close to myself and lifted her off her feet. For a second she was uncomfortable but then she smiled. I walked out of the water with her in my arms. While I was carrying her away from the water she noticed some shells on the sand. She requested me to let her go and I kept her down. She bent down and picked up a shell and gave it to me.

"What am I going to do with this?" I asked inspecting the shell in my hand.

"So you don't like collecting shells? Thank God!" And she took the shell back from me and threw it away.

I always thought collecting shells from the beach was stupid and fortunately she felt the same way. I just found out one more thing about her which I listed among those several others in the similar thoughts column between myself and Aditi. The list was getting longer every second and I kept falling for her more and more.

The hotel people had put cots and made sitting areas close to the beach and so I thought maybe we could sit there. I grabbed her hands and pulled her in front of me. I held both her hands in mine and put one of my feet forward for her to step on it. She realized what I was asking of her and she stepped on it. I pushed the second foot forward and while stepping on it she curved her hands around my neck and hugged me tight. I slowly started walking my feet and headed towards the cots made by the hotel people.

"Where are you going?" She asked while hugging me.

"I thought maybe we can sit over there and talk." I replied.

She got off my feet, turned around to check the place and then turned back towards me.

"You want to sit on those chairs with the umbrellas?" She enquired.

"So where do you want to sit?" I asked her.

She took a step back and adjusted herself to face the beach, folded her legs and sat down right there on the sand and said "How about here?"

"You want to sit here?" I asked again surprisingly.

She grabbed my hand and pulled me down to make me sit next to her. We were both facing the sun set. The sky was a shade of orange now. Far away near the horizon we could see small ships which were probably very large in their actual size. There were many birds flying in fleets in different directions but all we could see was black dots in the dark orange back ground. The whole scene looked more or less like a painting, us being the only live ones. The waves kept getting larger only to settle down and die at the shores. The sound of the waves dying and the water splashing at the shore was very romantic and caught our attention. I was watching the sun set in the far west while she was holding my arm with her head inclined on my shoulder witnessing the same. Soon the sun drowned and orange sky started turning dark making the moon appear from nowhere. Lights turned on at the top of the light house which was close in the vicinity. We turned around to see the entire hotel lit in lights of different colours and sizes. It was all very beautiful. We were having a perfect evening together and I loved the fact that she was enjoying my company.

After a short while one of the security guards came up and told us that the beach closes after 8 pm for safety reasons and we had to leave. The whole night was left ahead of us and I knew there was a lot of potential in the bedroom for things to go wrong. So I decided to stay out of it as much as possible. But our clothes were drenched and we had sand all over us. We needed to take a shower. We walked back to our villa together and she decided to go in first for the shower. While I waited for my turn I took my clothes out on the bed, the ones I was going to wear after the shower, and made a call to the reception. I heard the bathroom door unlock and she walked out drying her hair on the towel. I was picturing her in nice sexy lingerie or a silky night gown but she came out in a pair of pyjamas. Her cuteness was beyond limits leaving me speechless. She looked so much prettier with her wet hair that I had to comment. She was so fair that when she blushed it looked like we had painted her cheeks red.

"Go in and hurry up I'm hungry. Should I order from the room service or should I wait for you?" She asked.

"No don't order yet. We'll see when I come back ok." I replied.

I jumped out of the bed and hurried into the bathroom. I quickly took a shower and wrapped the towel around my waist and got out. She was still drying her hair and was surprised to see me topless. Her eyes widened and her cheeks turned red again.

"I'm a guy Aditi, its fine!" I exclaimed.

I put my clothes on and requested her to get ready to leave.

"Where are we going?" She enquired.

"Just get ready." I ordered her.

"But I don't have clothes Himanshu. There is only one pair left and that is for tomorrow. If I wear that now what will I wear tomorrow. Where are we going anyways?" She asked.

"We are going to the restaurant for dinner and I have something planned for you." I replied.

"No I can't go like this in my pyjamas. What will people think?" She was concerned.

I asked her to wait while I started searching for something in my bag.

"What are you looking for?" She asked.

"Turn around." I requested Aditi.

"What?" She asked widening her eyes.

"Just turn around and face the other side." I requested her again.

As she turned around in a confused mind I quickly changed into my shorts and a loose t-shirt.

"Come on now let's go." I said to Aditi.

She turned around and asked me how I was going to go out in shorts.

"Well I don't have pyjamas right now so you'll have to manage with these. Now get up and let us go." I ordered this time.

I grabbed her hands and pulled her out. We had left in such a hurry that we forgot to even wear our footwear. We walked all the way back to the side of the beach where there was a small table arranged for us. I had made the call to the manager for the arrangement and he had arranged it very well. She was shocked and surprised with her hands covering her mouth. I wrapped my arm around her and pushed her forwards. We met the manager half way and he asked me if the arrangement was as I had expected. I agreed and expressed my gratitude to him and had to push Aditi again who was still shocked. We walked closer to the spot and as we reached tears almost rolled out of her eyes.

There was a small round table with two chairs. There was a bunch of red roses lying here and there on the table with a small but bright candle lit in the centre of the table. The table was encircled by a set of 12 candles lamps and within this circle were petals of roses spread all over. Beyond this arrangement was the vast night sky filled with start and a half moon at the corner. The waves were still dying on the shore and made a louder cry. To spoil the entire view there was a waiter dressed in a suit to provide us with any assistance if required. I wished he wasn't there.

"How did you do all this?" She asked gasping for breath.

"I asked the manager to do me a favour." I replied.

"And he just agreed?" She was still surprised.

"No I had to lie. I told him that today was our 1st wedding anniversary and I wanted to make it special for you so he agreed." I explained.

"I love you!" She exclaimed and jumped towards me and hugged me so tight. After a moment I pushed myself off her arms and stepped into the circle and held my hand forward to invite her into it. She gently placed her hand on mine and stepped on the petals. I pulled her chair back and she placed herself with utmost manners. I took my seat and called the waiter. In the last few days I had learned about her likes and dislikes and so I felt free to order our supper without asking her.

"How may I help you sir?" The waiter asked.

"Get this pretty lady the best salad you have but without any meat and get me a chicken steak." I ordered.

"And how about some wine Aditi?" I asked.

"No. No alcohol. Please" She requested.

"Ok, get me coke please." I ordered the waiter.

The waiter left us alone there and we had a moment to ourselves.

"Don't we look ridiculous?" She asked.

"What do you mean?" I replied surprisingly.

"Come on Himanshu you made such an amazing arrangement and I'm dressed in pyjamas." She responded.

"Hello, I'm also wearing my shorts no?" I replied annoyingly.

"Yes that's what I'm saying. It would have been better no if you were all suited up and I was dressed in a gown?" She suggested.

"So you are saying that my shorts are spoiling the night?" I questioned her.

"No you dumbass, I'm just saying that this whole thing is amazing. I do not have words to describe it. I bet every girl in the entire world wants to be in my place right now." She said happily.

"You mean in your pyjamas." I asked sarcastically.

"No you idiot. Here with you!" She said tapping my head.

"Oh!" I acted surprised.

Soon the waiter served us with our supper and we were fighting battles with our knives and forks.

"I never told you I was a vegetarian. How did you know what to order for me?" She was puzzled.

"In the last 3 months we have met a total of 7 times and every single time you have ordered for something veg with a coke. Also every time I ordered for chicken you would make faces. It wasn't that big of a mystery to figure out you know." I elaborated.

"Alright. Now the dinner is done too. Tell me what other surprise you have for me." She asked smiling widely.

"I'd rather just surprise you instead of telling." I responded.

"So do it." She said.

I stood up from my chair and kneeled down in front of her.

"Oh my God. No." She exclaimed.

"I'm not proposing you for marriage you idiot. Just shut up and wait." I said loudly.

"Oh ok." She calmed down.

"Put your foot on my knee!" I ordered.

"What?" She asked surprisingly.

"Lift your right foot up and put it on my knee." I ordered again.

As soon as her soft sole touched my skin I reached to my right pocket and took out an anklet that I had bought for her. I put it around her ankle and asked her how it was.

She had a glimpse of it and stood off her chair. She pulled me up and hugged me tight.

"Oh wait." I said and grabbed my phone from the table and switched on a song on the loud speaker.

"Is it Kenny? Oh my God he is one of my favourite artists." She exclaimed.

"I'm sorry I could not arrange for a band but this is the best I could do." I apologized.

She just hummed and kept hugging me tighter.

"Would you dance with me Aditi?" I requested.

And there we were on the sea shore under the star filled night sky within the circle made of candle lamps wearing shorts and pyjamas, dancing to Kenny's music on those rose petals spread over the cold white sand with our naked feet.

"I don't think anything could make my day better." She confessed.

"Wait I have something else." I said.

"There is more? Nothing could be better than what you have done already Himanshu." She replied.

"Wait for this one." I requested her to close her eyes and then reached my left pocket and took out a small necklace made of unbroken complete shells which I had asked the manager to buy from the nearby local shops and get it for me.

I put it around her neck and tied it under her hair. She opened her eyes and touched the necklace with her gentle hands. She almost burst out in tears when she realized what it was.

"But how did you know I liked them?" She enquired.

"Aditi your eyes speak a lot. Earlier when you handed me the shell your eyes had expectations that I would like it. Then I denied and you threw it away and told me that you also hate it. But somewhere your eyes told me that you like shells and so I got this for you." I explained.

A tear rolled down her eye and she wrapped me around her arms. After a second she moved back and turned around to the waiter.

"Could you please give us a minute?"

He understood and left the area without a question. She turned to me again and this time wrapped her arms around my neck and lifted herself up on her toes.

Dr. Ravi Shekhar Krishna

"Himanshu?"

"Yes baby?"

"Kiss me."

"But I just had chicken."

"Kiss me already you dumbass."

"Are you sure?"

This time she didn't tell anything but instead pushed herself forward and locked her lips with mine. The touch of her lips was like a drug that ran through my lips into my entire body and soon I was knocked out. I couldn't even feel my heart beating. All I could sense was that my lips were still one with hers and she was hugging me tight. The background had no sound at all and it felt as if the waves had turned away from the shore.

After the entire day we both were so tired that there was no potential left for anything to happen on the bed. We both walked back to the room together and when we opened the door we were both surprised. The mess we had made was cleaned up and the room was dimly lit. The bed was decorated with red roses with a card in the centre which read "Happy Anniversary, hope you go on together forever."

We both looked at each other and smiled. She pulled me closer and pecked my lips and then fell on the bed.

"I'm really tired Himanshu." She said.

"So am I!" I confessed too.

"Come on. Get on the bed now. I need my pillow." She ordered me like she was my wife already.

As soon as I got on the bed she pulled my left arm out and shifted closer to me. She kept her head on my arm and hugged me from the side. I never felt so amazing before in my entire life. Now I realized what love was and how it felt. She was the girl of my dreams and I wasn't going to let her go. She went off to her dream world while I was busy thinking. I kissed her forehead gently and closed my eyes soon.

I woke up next morning with a pillow by my side. Aditi was all freshened up and dressed all ready to go.

"Hey good morning baby." She wished me.

"Hey what time is it?" I asked in my cranky voice.

"Its 10!" She replied.

"Its 10 am already?" I woke up in surprise.

"Yeah. You were sleeping like a little baby so I didn't want to wake you up." She explained.

"We have to leave soon." I got up from the bed in a hurry and ran inside the bathroom. Then I ran back out and pecked her on her cheeks and said "Hurry up baby, pack your bags. I'll get ready quickly ok. We have to leave."

"But where to?" She asked.

"I'll tell you on the way." I said while getting back into the bathroom.

When I stepped out of the bathroom she was all set to go. I quickly dressed myself up and packed my bag. I made a call to the reception to keep all the formalities ready. It was almost 12 by the time everything was settled and we left the resort.

"Where are we going Himanshu?" She asked me as we entered an auto.

"Do you like animation movies?" I asked.

"Yes I do! Are we going for Wall-E?" She asked with a smile.

"Yes we are!" That was the only good movie released during that month and we didn't have any other good options. There was only one show playing at this theatre on MG road but I wasn't sure if we would make it in time.

"That's so sweet of you." She replied.

"Let's just hope we make it in time." I was worried.

There was a lot of traffic that day and unfortunately we were late for the movie. It was already almost 1.30 pm by the time we reached. Another movie was not an option because by the time it got over, it would be past 5 pm and I had to drop Aditi back to the hostel before 6 pm. So instead we decided to go pizza hut that was close by for lunch. We had our tummies full with pasta and deserts. I paid the bill and we walked to the auto stand. She told the driver the directions to her hostel and we headed that way. We both got off near her hostel and just stood on the footpath for a while. The entire weekend was over already but I wasn't satisfied. I was ready to spend the rest of my life with this girl and she was going to go away in some time. There was no smile on either of our faces.

"So I should get going now?" She spoke.

"Yeah I guess." I replied.

"Won't you ask me to stay?" She asked me eagerly.

"I really want to but I know you have to go back to the hostel." I said sadly.

"Yes I do!" She said turning her face away.

"So we'll meet again soon?" I asked.

"Of course we will. Hey I have something for you. I totally forgot about it. But you have to promise that you will accept it. You cannot deny it ok." She started digging into her bag.

"But what is it?" I asked.

"I am not going to tell you. Promise me that you will accept it. Please?" She requested.

I agreed and she took out an envelope and handed it over to me.

I opened it and started looking for what it was.

"I'm really sorry Himanshu. I didn't know that our stay would be so expensive. I mean I didn't know you had planned so much for us. I was really surprised." She explained.

"This is ridiculous Aditi. Did I ask you for anything?" I almost yelled at her trying to hand her back the three thousand rupees she had put in the envelope.

"No Himanshu. Why do you have to spend on the entire thing when we equally shared the happiness? This time I could save only this much and I'm really sorry about that. Next time will be all on me. Moreover you promised that you wouldn't deny it. So shut up now and put it in your pocket." She ordered me.

I quietly put it in my pocket and asked her "So there is going to be a next time?"

"Yes there will be many next times! But you'll have to figure out new ways to surprise me." She said placing her palm on my chest.

"Leave that to me. Now go inside your hostel. These people around here are giving us those weird stares." I gestured at the surrounding people and said.

She shook hands with me and started walking away.

I wish she had stayed. I wished she never had to leave. I wish she was mine forever. I stood there till she got into her hostel. I turned around after she left my vicinity and got into an auto and asked him to drive me to my hostel. A few minutes later my phone buzzed with Aditi's message.

"Thr is sumthin else in d envelpe fr my baby. It isnt tht gr8 bt I hope u lyk it. ☺"

I opened the envelope again and found a paper folded twice on itself. On opening it I was surprised at first but then I smiled. It was for the first time that someone had written a poem for me.

I know this whiz kid

He is such a witty kid

Jokes, teases and talks sense

You'll love the loving way he loves his friends

He'll pull your leg when he gets the chance

He rocks the stage, boy he can dance

He always says he sucks at singing

No one knows how, but he keeps on winning

He has this kiddish face, don't know since when

He towers to a height of five feet eleven

An ace at sports, especially basketball

He plays, even if he gets hurt or fall

Though way too cute like an angelic honey bun

This one baby is way too stubborn

He'll go to any extent in order to win

No matter how much you coax him, he'll never take his medicine

A characteristic feature is his cylindrical shape

And his husky voice that I've caught on tape

He is one hell of a lazy goose

He gets real crazy when he loses his fuse

He's got this nick name "chipmunk"

I'm planning to switch that to plain old skunk

Ok, ok, that was rude but the fault isn't mine

I simply couldn't come up with a more appropriate rhyme.

Love, Aditi.

Chapter Twenty

"THE CALL"

The week end was over and all I was left with were the thoughts of my better half. The entire day I kept thinking about her. She told me that we were going to meet again and so I was thinking of new ideas on how to surprise her the next time we meet. This is why I was so lost when my name was called out by Dr. Kamal sir in class. Apparently I had passed in community medicine paper and people weren't ready to believe that. BD, Rajesh and Suraj dragged me down to the department to check my answer sheet when I got the text that drastically changed my thoughts. It was Reena's text which read "Cn u meet me nw, in the juice stal?"

This was the first time in weeks when I thought about her. She had gone home after her exams and I was so lost with Aditi that I had forgotten about her. I had to confess to her about Aditi and that I could not go on with her like this. So I replied "Whn did u come bak? Evn I hv sumthin very important to tel u! Wil b thr in 5!"

But when I met her I found things to be complicated more than my imagination. She had failed her anatomy paper and was totally depressed about it. We spoke about it and I tried to console her but there was more that was bothering her. We went to her house and she opened up to me. She described the whole picture at her house to me and even I was moved. She was going through a lot at one go. First the exams and then her parents, it would have been too much to handle. Breaking up with her would have devastated her completely at this moment and so I decided to keep my feelings to myself.

A week passed by and I still found myself stuck between both of them struggling to find a solution and quick. Soon I learned that Reena cleared her re-evaluation and that would have been a good enough opportunity to tell her everything. Yes she would have been heartbroken if I had told her but I didn't have an option. But even that day things went exactly opposite of how I wanted them to. I reached Reena's house to tell her that she passed and hopefully open up to her but at her door was her mother who welcomed me in. There was no smile on her face and neither was on Reena's when I met her in her bedroom. She burst out into a river of tears when she hugged me and I learned that her parents were splitting up. She was broken down and there was nobody other than me who could help her right now. She was dependent on me and leaving her at this moment would be an act of cruelty and I wasn't so heartless.

It had been over a month that the divorce news was broken to Reena. She seemed to be coping well with the whole situation and even better, she was dealing with the second year much better than how I did. And the thoughts of me opening up to her started bothering me again. So just like any other day I asked her to meet me at the juice stall after classes.

"Hey, so what was this important thing you wanted to talk to me about?" She asked placing herself on the seat opposite to me.

"Let us order something to eat first? I'm hungry!" I declared.

We both got our orders and sat in front of each other.

"So tell me how your day was?" I enquired.

"It was ok. That Brigadier Philip tried really hard to tell us how to take a case history but we disappointed him like always. It was fun though. How was your day?" She asked.

"Yeah it was ok." I replied.

213

This way our conversation kept going on and on for over an hour when she realized it was time for her to go back to the hostel. At many times I tried to tell her how I felt but i just couldn't bring myself up to tell her on her face. I was really scared. So i thought maybe I'll confess to her over the phone and requested her to call me around 8 pm.

I walked back to the hostel in despair thinking about the whole thing. How can I tell her the entire thing? Will she understand? What if she doesn't? All these thoughts ran away when I heard my phone ringing. I checked my watch to learn it was only 7 pm. Why was Reena calling me so early?

I picked up the phone and got blasted by Reena. What I didn't want happened! I didn't want her to get hurt this badly but she had to learn it the hard way. Even while she was yelling at me all I could think of was Aditi. I was only hoping that Aditi had not found out about me and Reena because if that had happened then I would lose her for sure and that was something I would never have wanted to happen. I knew I had hurt Reena really badly but there was nothing more that I could have done but to say sorry. But she just yelled at me, ended up crying and kept the phone even before I could say anything.

I typed in Aditi's number to call her but my phone rang before I could dial her number. I picked up and in a shivering voice answered the call. In a split second I realized Aditi wasn't mine anymore. Things had gone wrong both ways and I was the one who was the reason for it. I could have ended it before but I couldn't. I didn't. I knew if had continued things would end up in a mess like this. Even then I let it go on. The entire fault was mine and only mine. There was only one person for me to curse and that was me. I hated myself to the core. Tears started rolling down my eyes and they were not going to stop anytime soon. I tried calling Aditi again and telling her the truth but she kept rejecting my calls. While I was trying to call Aditi repeatedly I received a text from Reena.

"Wat did I evr do so rng 2 u tht u hurt me so bad? N u dnt evn hv d courtesy 2 gimme an explanatn! I hate u Himanshu. I hate u!"

This is when it struck me again that Aditi was not the only one who was traumatized. I had to take care of both the sides but I could do that only if they let me. I tried calling Reena few times but now even she was rejecting all my calls. I tried calling Aditi few more times again but still no luck. I got fed up of cursing and blaming myself and trying to call both of them. I decided to send them both a text and end it for good.

I sat down on my bed crossing my legs after wiping the tears off my face. And then I started typing.

Message to Aditi

"I knw u dnt wana hear frm me agn bt i hv to say sumthing so plz read d rest wid a peaceful mind. I knw i cnt evn justify all tht hs happend. Yes it ws my fault bt i cudnt do anything abt it. I wantd to let go of Reena n stay wid u. It ws always u Aditi n nt her. U wer the girl i wantd n if i cud go bak in time i wd do evrythin tht i cn to make things ryt btw us. I knw ur hurt n i hate myself fr bringing u this pain bt i need u to knw tht im realy realy sorry. I knw u dnt wana tok to me evr agn n evn i knw tht im nt worthy enuf. U deserve much much bettr Aditi. So im leaving n im nvr gona bothr u agn. Bt jst so tht u knw, i realy loved u, i stil do n always wil. Gudbye Aditi.

Message to Reena

I knw things r nt goin the way u wanted. Life is always a mess n it'l always b difficult. U cant run away frm tht. I ws a rng turn u took n im sorry i hd to happen in ur life. I always wantd to tel u the truth bt things never workd out. Moreovr if things wer fine in ur family thn mayb u wdnt hv been so attached to me. Leavin possibilities aside im realy sorry fr evrythin tht went rng. V r in the same colge n i knw u'l hv to face me sumwhr bt i assure u tht i'l try nt to make things wrse fr u. I hope things improve on ur side. Once agn im realy realy sorry. Tc

After this I never heard from either of them again.

215

Chapter Twenty One

"STAND UP AND SALUTE"

After the exams I had come home for a few weeks. Most of my viva had gone silent from my side but surprising I had passed in all the three subjects. Even though it was a second class and I just made it through, a pass was a pass and that was good enough for my dad. Although he sure was suspicious about what had gone wrong with me. Mom used to make all my favourite dishes every single day but I had the least interest in eating. There were many occasions when my parents tried asking me what was wrong with me but I had nothing to tell them. Even if I had the courage to open up to them I would never have known how to tell them what I had done. Soon the vacation was over and I carried my depression back to the hostel. I was least interested in any of the activities happening around. The cheerful funny me was lost somewhere and the lonely depressed me was ruling all over my soul. Even though I did not want to attend a single class I was forced to as low attendance percentage could restrain me from writing my final university exams. So I somehow used to push myself to the classes even though I never paid attention. Almost 6 month of posting was over and I had not even opened my mind in any of the classes. Soon the semester exams came and passed me by like a breeze of cold air and I failed in all four subjects. I was called in by the head of all the departments and counselled as I was one among the least scorers in all the four subjects. Even my parents were called and informed regarding my performance which increased there anxiousness and tension by multiple folds. I repeatedly got calls from home asking for what was wrong with me but I still had no answer.

Even my friends were bothered with my altered behaviour for they had never seen this me. Suraj came to my room one day and enquired about how things were going on with me and all I could say was that I was holding on somehow. He realized something was bothering me a lot which was also the same reason why I was screwing up in college. After further queries with me he realized he could not have taken the answer out of my mouth so he tried to help me in other ways.

"It's been ages since you have attended clinics Himanshu. We have OBG posting starting from tomorrow and you are coming with me to the OPD. I'll pick you up from your room at 7.45 am." He almost ordered.

"Fine!" I replied as if I didn't even hear him.

Even I was bored sitting in my room all day for so long that I decided to go. I got up at 7 am and got of my bed to go to the washroom. BD barged into the room with his towel around his waist dripping wet in water and was surprised to see me this early.

"Are you going to college in time today? Wow!" BD exclaimed.

"Just shut up ok." I told BD.

"You are going to the bathroom now right? Here is your soap!" Saying that he handed me my soap.

"Why did you have it?" I asked.

"My soap got over so I thought I'll use yours." He explained.

"And how long has it been?" I enquired.

"Two days I guess. I keep forgetting to buy me a new one." He replied.

"Two days? Are you kidding me? You better get a new soap for yourself today itself!" I ordered him.

"Don't use that tone with me! What if I don't buy a new one? What will you do?" He threatened me.

"Well tomorrow morning when you take my soap just think of the last place I wash and the first place you rub it on!" I told BD.

"Oh is it so? I get up before you Himanshu so maybe you should think of that!" He replied.

"Damn it!" I reached for my wallet and ran down to the store to buy a new soap. As I came back to my room BD was about to leave.

"Oh thanks for getting me a new soap." BD said.

"It's not for you asshole. You can keep mine. I'm going to use this one now." I responded.

"Fine! That works for me!" And he left with a smile on his face.

I quickly got ready and left with Suraj at the right time for the OBG department. We attended the morning class at 8 am and for almost an hour I found myself controlling myself not to sleep. After the class we were supposed to go for the practical part of the posting. That meant going to the labour room and I wasn't ready for that considering my last experience in there wasn't so good, even though it was a year ago. So Suraj decided to take me to the ultrasound room because he was sure that if he left me unattended I would bunk to come back to the hostel. We entered the scan room with a bunch of 4 or 5 girls of our batch. It was dimly lit room with a bed in the middle and a scan machine next to it. Under the machine there was a small box which looked almost full. I looked closer to find what it was full of and was surprised to learn that it was condoms. Yes that box was filled with used condoms. I was a little embarrassed for some reason and started looking here and there. While wandering my eyes I caught attention to the box that was kept behind the scan machine on a table that was full too. But this time it was brand new condoms. Soon a professor walked in with a young female patient and ordered her to lie down on the bed. The assisting sister helped the patient to undress and when she got on to the bed she was only wearing her kurta. The professor picked up a probe of the scan machine which was at least ten inches long and the sister grabbed a condom and opened it up. The professor pointed the probe towards the sister and she put on the condom over the probe in a jiffy. The professor ordered the patient to spread her legs and she just stuck that long probe covered with a condom inside her. The girls standing in front of me had no reaction at all but I was feeling very uncomfortable. Even Suraj who stood by my side had an expression less face. So I also thought this was a very regular thing and I went along with it. But a few seconds later something happened that made everyone in the room uncomfortable. The patient who had a ten inches long probe stuck inside of her started moaning. And it wasn't just moaning in pain, it sounded like she was enjoying it. This made all of us students feel uncomfortable. Soon the professor emptied her cavity and the moaning stopped abruptly. The young patient got up from the bed with a disappointed face as if she was about to but couldn't.

I requested Suraj to leave with me from that scan room as I couldn't have taken another girl moaning because of a machine. That thought was just disturbing. Suraj agreed and I started searching for the door in that dark room.

"Hey Himanshu, wait for a second." Suraj requested.

"What happened? Dude what are you doing?" I asked surprisingly.

Suraj had stepped in close to the new condoms box and was digging in for a few. While the sister wasn't watching he quickly grabbed a couple of them and slid his hand in his pocket and walked to wards me.

"What the fuck was that Suraj?" I asked.

"What are you talking about Himanshu?" He responded.

"Come on dude I'm not blind." I replied.

"I just want to know how it feels." He said.

"How it feels to have sex with a condom on?" I asked.

"No, how it feels to put it on!" He explained his curiosity.

"You have never used a condom before?" I asked again.

"No! What's the big deal?" He asked.

"You are telling me that you have been in a relationship for the last 3 years and you have never used a condom?" I asked surprisingly.

"So?" He asked.

"So nothing! Let us go." I said and opened the door.

We left the scan room and I convinced him to let me bunk the rest of the day. I did go to the afternoon lectures but as usual I either slept off or was lost in my thoughts.

That night my brother called me. This was something unusual. I didn't even remember the last time we spoke properly. Even though I was very close and opened up to him about everything, we were both the reserved kind of guys when it came to personal issues, which was probably the reason why I never sought his help in my case. In a confused state I picked up his phone.

"Hello?"

"What the fuck is wrong with you? Do you know how much mom and dad are bothered about you? Either you are going to tell me who that girl is and what went wrong or I'm telling mom and dad!" He threatened me straight away.

"How did you know about Aditi?" I asked surprisingly.

"So that's her name?" He responded.

"But how did you know it was because of a girl?" I was still in shock.

"I'm your elder brother Himanshu. I've been through rough times too. Now tell me what went wrong with you and Aditi." He asked.

I narrated him the entire story and told him how I was the reason for my own depression. He tried to console me a lot but nothing seemed to be working. But the last few things he said about this topic were something that hit me.

"Let me make it simple and clear to you Himanshu. You like this girl a lot and clearly you care too much that you decided to let her go and not bother her again. Girls are not that dumb. She will realize things sooner or later. Trust me on that. All you need is a little spark that is going to start up things between you guys again. And don't be an idiot and start roaming around her hostel or college because that is going to piss her off. Just wait for the right moment. I'm sure you'll get lucky like always. But this time when things get started, don't you dare screw up because if you do I'm going to come there personally and kick your butt."

I hummed with a smile and he went on.

"Well the other reason why I called you was because there was something I needed to tell you. My marriage is fixed. Mom and dad didn't know how to tell you so they asked me to tell you. I know your exams are in two months and that's why I made sure that not a single function is kept in these two months. Dates are not fixed yet and neither am I sure about this decision but the engagement will be soon after your exams so you should be prepared. I know you wouldn't get time during your exams so go out and get yourself some good clothes and suits if possible because most probably you'll be landing at the function right after your exams get over. So be prepared. Ok?"

"Yes bhaiya."

"Now go on and study something. Screwing up results because of a girl was something that I did too, and that only made me lose 6 precious months of my life and that is something that I regret till date. Even I have to go to the hospital now so I'll catch up with you later ok. And if I get another complaint from mom and dad about you I'm going to kill you. And I am not kidding!" and the call ended.

All the things that my brother told me struck my mind a little bit. That night I opened my book for the first time after almost 6 months. BD walked in and was surprised and immediately called Suraj and few people in the corridor to witness this once in a lifetime happening. I cursed them and called them names and asked them to get lost. Even over the next few days I started paying attention in class and Aditi seemed to bother me less. The only exams left were the final universities that were due in 3 weeks. Only two more working days were left for us and I had to pick a suit for myself for my brother's engagement. I asked a lot of people to go out with me to help me pick the suit but every one gave me the excuse of studies. I finally found Raunak who was ready to come with me and we bunked the 2nd last day of our college and headed to the wedding centre on MG road to get me a suit. It was a seven storied building and the men's section was on the 6th and the women's jewellery section was just above us, which made finding the elevators empty, very difficult. We browsed through a lot of suits and Raunak made me try many of them on before we finalised on two. We went to the counter to pay but were handed over a token instead and were told that we will have to pick up our material on the ground floor at the cash counter. This time Raunak was not willing to use the stairs and so we waited for the elevator. The elevators had a glass door which made everything inside the elevator visible to the crowd. When I pressed on the button a lift started descending down from the 7th floor and I could see everyone inside. There was this tall dark man, probably in his mid-forties standing stiff and strong. The only thing that probably made him look vulnerable was the girl he was hiding behind that huge figure who was probably her daughter. But I couldn't see her properly. She was wearing a red skirt and a black top and had her hair open and long. She resembled my Aditi a lot especially with her dressing sense and the simplicity that she wore. I had a glimpse of her hand and realized she was as fair as Aditi and suddenly my heart started pounding harder. The door opened and Raunak pushed me forwards. I walked past the huge figure with my eyes closed and my heart almost stopped beating for a second. I had a glimpse of that pretty face and took a breath of relief. It wasn't Aditi. I wished she was but she wasn't. Yes, this girl was very pretty. Her eyes were big and beautiful and she had a very good sense of clothing. But she wasn't my Aditi. I ignored the pretty girl and stood next to her when the door of the elevator closed. It started descending again and so did my thought into the lake of my past. I was totally lost in my thoughts when something caught my eye. As the elevator came to a stop I swear my heart did too. My lungs refused to breath. My eye lids refused to fall. My limbs refused to move. People from the elevator got out and the people waiting for the elevator got in but two pairs of legs didn't move at all. One was mine and the other pair was hers. Our eyes met and locked. The rest of the background went blur when I saw her. The chattering people around suddenly quieted down and I almost heard her breath. It was her. It was my Aditi!

"Himanshu lets go, what are you waiting for?" Raunak's voice tried to distract me.

"Aditi the door would close soon and I'm not going to wait for you." A girl next to me screamed.

Her eyes broke the lock and her feet moved forward. I struggled hard to breath and then pushed myself out of the elevator. She passed by me barely brushing my shoulder. I did not dare to turn back. She was the love of my life but I was the one who made her life miserable. I stared at my feet while I walked to the counter. I paid the bill, Raunak picked up the bags and we left the store soon. I did not want to think about Aditi. I had just got back into my senses. Recently I had opened my books and I did not want to screw up my exams and add 6 more months to my miserable college life. I held my own hand strong and convinced myself that Aditi was not going to bother me at all. But just like always my phone buzzed at the wrong times.

"Omg!!" A text message read.

It was from Aditi. But I had decided not to let her affect me. So I chose not to respond to her. We got back to the hostel and I thanked Raunak for accompanying me. I reached my room and after changing and settling down, opened my books and sat down on my study table. I tried harder and harder to push Aditi off my thoughts and concentrate on the subject but failed miserably. Many at times I picked up my phone to text her back but I somehow controlled myself and pushed the phone away. Fighting her thoughts hanging somewhere between my books and my love I drifted off to sleep on my table.

BD woke me up at 7.30 in the morning and asked me if I was going to attend the last class of our entire college life. That was something I could not have said no to. I got up immediately and requested him to wait for me while I got ready. We both left the hostel soon and split at the hospital entrance as he had medicine class by Dr Reddy and I was going to attend the last case discussion by our Brigadier.

As we were told, the Brigadier walked in exactly at 10 am and closed the door behind him. "Good morning doctors" roared to every corner of the room and all of us stood up to wish him.

"Take your seats and my lady, start the presentation." He ordered.

Janani was the girl who was presenting the last case of the year and most of us were excited that we wouldn't have to face most of our professors. But only few of us had realized how much we were going to miss our classes. The case presentation started very well and went on without any disruption. She was presenting a case of hernia and had studied a lot for it was the last day. The Brigadier was impressed so far and we saw a smile on his face which was a rare occasion. Soon she was done with her examination of the patient part and took a pause for Brigadier to comment.

"Madam, I will surely say that you have done a good job with the presentation so far. But only because it is a case of hernia, it does not mean that you forget the examination of the genital region, it is equally important. So why don't you enlighten us about that?" He spoke.

Her face showed a smile when the brigadier started, but when he asked her for the genital examination her facial expressions made it obvious that she had not read that part.

"Go on madam." He commanded this time.

With a lot of hesitation she started, but brigadier objected soon.

"External genital examination—Penis is normal in size" Janani hesitantly started.

"Normal in size? Madam they come in different sizes and most of them appear normal according to the person who is looking at it. What is normal according to you?" He interrupted Janani with an evil smile on his face.

We were all stunned for such a statement. For obvious reasons Janani kept quiet and the brigadier ignored the mistake and asked her to continue.

"On moving it left it moves left, on moving it right it moves right." Now what she was probably trying to do was to explain the mobility of a swelling, in this case the penis. Even though it wasn't necessary she said it out loud only to hear another amazing comment from the brigadier.

He laughed out loud and said "Madam if you move it left and right like that, it will stand up and salute you!"

At this moment we forgot that he was a Brigadier and all of us burst out into laughter. We were laughing so hard that some of the people outside the class room tried to look inside to see what was happening. Janani was embarrassed and almost filled her eyes with tears. The brigadier realized that she was about to burst out into tears and tried to control the situation.

My lady, please have a seat. And all of you idiots shut up and listen.

With that heavy voice of his, the whole room went silent. Janani took a seat in the front row and the brigadier explained to us the examination of genital system in details. On that last day we learned two things, one was the examination of the genital system and second was the fact that even the heart of an army man melts down in front of a woman's tears.

Chapter Twenty Two

"I WAS LOST, YOU FOUND ME"

As it was the last day of college, most of the student decided to go to the juice stall and enjoy. Suraj tagged me along with him and even though I was not very social person at the given point of time, I had to go. Just when I was about to forget everything and start having fun my phone buzzed and I slipped back into my state of depression.

"Do u generally ignore people like this or is it jst me?"

It was Aditi's message. The more hurtful part was that it was the same message which she had sent me when we had actually started talking a year ago. After trying desperately for almost half an hour I failed to control myself and replied to her text.

"Hey, Im surprisd u still remembr me."

"Hw wd I evr frgt u Himanshu?" She replied.

"Ya thts true, i mean no1 hs evr put u thru wat i hv done ryt?" I replied.

"Nw dnt start up on tht. Cal me whn ur free k?" Her reply came.

I got up from my table and informed Suraj that I was leaving because I had to make a call. I quickly ran out the juice stall and reached the hostel soon. I took my phone out in the corridor itself and called her.

"Hey, how are you Himanshu?" She asked.

"I'm fine." I replied.

"Are you really?" She asked in a rough tone.

"Yes I am!" I tried to be stern.

"But I didn't hear many things about you being fine. Instead of what I have heard it seems like you are all messed up." She replied.

"What did you hear?" I asked.

"I heard about your semester exams and how you failed all of them miserably." She answered.

"Who told you that?" I asked again.

"That doesn't matter. What matters is that your life is in your hands and you are screwing it up." She spoke.

"Why do you care so much?" I questioned her.

"What do you mean I care so much? Do you even know how much you meant to me?" She was now angry.

I kept silent.

"Get this one thing in your head Himanshu, you better not fail your final exams, because if you do I'm going to come there and bang your head on the wall myself." She almost screamed.

For the first time in the last six months I smiled properly. Even though it was for banging my head on the wall, it did make my lips widen.

We both went on with the conversation about her college and then how things were going with our families. She was happy to hear about my brother's engagement and to share the news of her brother's selection in some company in Australia. We both shared a lot of details, about almost everything that we had missed out on in the last one year. Soon it was time for dinner and she had to leave.

"Before I keep the phone I need you to promise me something Himanshu. Would you?" She asked.

"What is it?" I asked.

"You have to promise me that you are going to study well and clear your exams. I don't want to see you waste another six months of your life in that stupid college. Promise me Himanshu!" She requested.

"I promise!" I replied.

"Good boy! Now go and study. And listen, if ever you need to talk to someone, know that I'm here for you ok." She said.

"Thanks Aditi." I replied.

"Now go have dinner and then study!" She ordered me.

"Yes madam." I replied.

"Bye." She said with a giggle and kept the phone.

All of a sudden this fire started within me. The entire year that I spent wasting my time did come as regret to me but I was determined to use the next two weeks of my preparation leave very well. I skipped dinner as usual and sat down on my study table. I turned the pages of my book and put my ear phones on. After few minutes BD came in and acted very surprised. He walked back out of the room and got back in and asked.

"Did I enter the wrong room?"

"No this is our room only. Why what happened?" I asked.

"You are studying!" BD replied.

"Yes, so?" I asked getting annoyed.

"No it wasn't a question! I meant you are studying! Like a surprised statement you idiot. Anyways this motivates me to watch a movie." BD said.

"How does me studying make you want to watch a movie?" I enquired.

"I don't know. I just needed an excuse to watch a movie. You are studying today so I will watch a movie." BD said.

"Your wish BD!" And I pulled my ear phones back on and drowned into my book again.

Days went on and so did my studies. I used to get saturated very often and every time when it happened my phone used to dial just one number. We used to talk for a few minutes and then she would push me back to studies. Having her around was the best and the only thing that was working for me. Soon the preparation leave reached its dead line and I started freaking out more. But there was only one person who knew how to cool me down and bring peace to my mind. Even after every exam the first thing I used to do was to call her and tell her how the paper was. She used to listen to me and then prepare me well for the next paper. I was so dependent on her that I couldn't even think of anything else at that moment, including talking to my parents. The only time I realized that I hadn't spoken to my parent for ages was when my exams were done and I was about to board the flight for my departure from Kochi. Even then the last call I made before switching off my phone was to Aditi. I convinced her that just because I was going home didn't mean that I would stop texting her as it happened in her case a year ago.

As soon as the flight landed I switched on my phone and texted Aditi. We started having a chat and a smile anchored itself on my lips. I collected my luggage and headed out. This time mom and dad both had come to pick me up. For some reason they both had a very surprised look on their faces. They both kept giving me those questioning looks even after I hugged both of them. We got into the car and before mom could say anything I asked for the boxes of homemade food that she always gets for me. While I was hogging on those delicious foods both of them kept pin drop silence and so I had to ask them.

"Why are you guys so surprised?"

"We are not surprised? Are you surprised?" My dad asked my mom.

"A little bit maybe." Mom replied.

"But why?" Dad asked.

"The last time my son came home, he didn't even eat properly, forget talking to us and smiling. I think we have picked up somebody else by mistake." Mom said to my Dad.

"Oye there is nothing like that. Tell me how my sister in law is. I haven't even seen her picture. And when is the engagement." I enquired.

"The dates were postponed to next month because your mother wanted it according to some religious days." Dad explained.

"So what is wrong in that? I only want things to work out better for Raj." Mom clarified.

"But how can you be so superstitious. Even we ran away and got married on a Sunday. I think we have done pretty well holding on to each other for 32 years now." Dad justified his side.

"Yes that is true but that doesn't mean you call me superstitious." Mom was getting annoyed.

"But you are superstitious." Dad declared.

This way the argument went on between my parents while I got busy texting Aditi. Soon we reached home and my normal schedule of eating sleeping eating movies sleeping and eating started again.

Finally the day of the results had arrived and there I was sitting in front of the computer waiting for my results. It had been over a month that I and Aditi had started talking again but there were no signs of things getting back to the way they were the first time we met. We were just friends as of now and even though I wanted things to get better and closer, there was nothing that I could have done. Like always my mind started wandering into stupid thoughts and I started getting scared. She had not messaged me since morning today. Usually my day started with her message every single day but today it never came. What if she came back just for my exams when she learned that I was screwing up big time. What if she found someone else better than me? What if she quit on me for no reason, I mean she had one big enough reason already.

"Dude the result is out. Go check yours." BD sent a chat.

My veins collapsed and all the blood was sucked out of my brain. For a second I felt that I was throwing an absent seizure. I somehow controlled myself and entered my registration number. But I was really scared to press the enter button for that would tell me my fate. And then my phone buzzed and eased my muscles.

"Hey buddy, heard ur results r out. No1 told me yet bt im sure u r a doc nw. Go check it out n buz me asap!"

That message relaxed my soul so much that I wasn't scared of the results anymore. Of course I wanted to pass but that fear wasn't there anymore.

I pressed the enter button and it was only a few seconds that my result would flash on the screen. In that second my heart skipped a beat, and a million things popped in my head. I was disturbed yet much focused.

I was lost still very stable. I had the love of my life with me but I still didn't have her. In that second I wished for many things, for my parents to be happy, for myself to pass but most importantly, for Aditi to not let go of me!

I WAS LOST . . . . YOU FOUND ME!!!

So lost was I, in this dreaded place

Doomed in this hell on earth

The dark of loneliness spreading all over

Smile and happiness losing its girth

No souls to give me company

Not even a single mate I could call my own

On this sturdy road of my miserable life

I was struggling all alone

The only saviour I could hope for

Was there up above

Though his existence was uncertain

I knelt and prayed and asked for love

Handpicked from his bunch of enchanted angels

God summoned one down to my relief

To bring back light in my darkened life

To help me win faith in my own belief

With her first stride into my world

My life took a turn

With a spark of her divine soul

My darkest fears started to run

With a spell of her magical wand

She blossomed, the flowers of joy

In her shield of pure love I was protected

And my fears stayed far away

She changed my entire being

Taught me how to smile, how to love

She became my friend, my companion

She was truly a gift sent from above

She was the blessing I needed

To become the man I always wanted to be

And now that her purpose seemed served

She is getting ready to leave

With her first step out of my life

My darkest fears grow strong again

Without her in my life

I'm sure to get lost . . . again

So I kneel in front of you, again and pray

Please don't let her let go of me

For I've realized my darkest fear

Is losing her and not the lonely me!!

THE END!